Time-slip, Graham Dunstan Martin's second fantasy novel, is set in Scotland in the twenty-first century. Edinburgh has been spared from total destruction in the holocaust and the society that exists has undergone dramatic changes. They survive in protective radiation suits. This is no ordinary holocaust novel. As in his well-received *Soul Master,* Dunstan Martin explores the themes of good and evil, of power and politics and (centrally) of religion.

At the centre of the novel is Jenny Blinkbonny, a teacher troubled in her mind and faith. She becomes intractably involved with Peter Gilchrist who has a passionate faith in his own powers of survival and believes it is his destiny to change the world. Gilchrist confronts the issues of guilt and despair in powerful preaching and moves to set the people free.

First they must remove their radsuits...

ORION

By the same author

The Soul Master

TIME-SLIP

GRAHAM DUNSTAN MARTIN

London
UNWIN PAPERBACKS
Boston   Sydney

ORION

UNWIN ® PAPERBACKS
40 Museum Street, London WC1A 1LU, UK

Unwin Paperbacks
Park Lane, Hemel Hempstead, Herts HP2 4TE, UK

Allen & Unwin Australia Pty Ltd
8 Napier Street, North Sydney,
NSW 2060, Australia

Unwin Paperbacks with the
Port Nicholson Press
PO Box 11-838 Wellington, New Zealand

First published in Unwin Paperbacks 1986

British Library Cataloguing in Publication Data

Martin, Graham Dunstan
    Time-slip.
    I. Title
    823'.914[F]   PR6063.A714/

    ISBN 0-04-823284-X

Set in Cheltenham Book by A. J. Latham, Dunstable

Printed and bound in Great Britain by
Hazell, Watson & Viney Limited,
Aylesbury, Bucks

To
Denis
Demonpion

Contents

		page
Prologue		1
1	Lord, Let Me in the Lifeboat	3
2	Really the Blues	22
3	Always, All Alone and Stumbling	33
4	I Told You Once, I Told You Twice	38
5	Where Am I?	48
6	That Old Black Magic	57
7	Easy Rider	65
8	Dear Old Southland	72
9	'T Ain't No Sin	84
10	Ole Miss	92
11	There'll Be Some Changes Made	97
12	Jelly Roll Blues	106
13	High Society	113
14	Blood on the Moon	117
15	Baby Won't You Please Come Home?	125
16	After You've Gone	135
17	When the Saints Go Marching In	141
18	Slipping and Sliding	150
	Epilogue	160

Who sees with equal eye, as God of all,
A hero perish, or a sparrow fall,
Atoms or systems into ruin hurled,
And now a bubble burst, and now a world.
Alexander Pope

Author's Note

This is a tale of fantasy and foreboding, and none of the characters in it resembles any real human being, alive or dead — though I cannot, of course, speak for those as yet unborn.

Prologue

*Shall there be evil in a city, and
the Lord hath not done it?*

——— AMOS 3:6 ———

Edinburgh, 26 July 2053

At the East end of St Mary's Cathedral, under Gilbert Scott's three lofty spires, shaped like a triune reflection of the same absolute certainty, there hangs an enormous tapestry, thirty feet in height. The image upon it is not that of Christ — or at least not that of Jesus hanging upon His cross — but of a modern Christ, his eyes closed, his arms crossed like an Egyptian Pharaoh, a blissful unsmiling calm upon his face, and a scarlet hole in his forehead. Behind him, to right and left, are two further images of the same figure, but vague, like ghosts. Each of these has his eyes open and is smiling. Two living shadows and a dead reality.

'For it is written,' cries the preacher on his platform, ' "The one shall be taken and the other left." '

The congregation thronging the building repeat these words in a vast and ringing shout. The echo, refracted off pillars, arches and walls, comes bouncing back, then spreads out into a blur of repeated sounds, as if it represents different realities, none of them quite simultaneous.

' "For His yoke is easy, His burden is light." '

At the front of the audience, women are weeping openly, among them Jenny Gilchrist, 'Mother' of the Kirk.

'Today,' says the minister, 'on this 26th day of July 2053, we mourn the prophet and martyr Peter Gilchrist, founder of the Kirk, finder of the secret of good and evil. On this very day ten years ago he was wickedly done to death by the heathen — murdered in the presence of a hundred thousand worshippers. His blood still cries like Abel's from the ground ...'

1

The minister points to a section of planking erected beside the pulpit, on which can be seen a dark stain shaped something like a candelabra. Unkind tongues are known to claim that the stain is not blood, but paint, for surreptitious penknives often prise out fragments of the original to be used as lucky charms.

'Yet our yoke is easy, our burden is light. We know that in Ifwhere, our dear Lord and Master is still alive, still preaching his holy message. Let us remind ourselves of his teaching. We are the first society in history where nobody is afraid. Where the Universe is known to be good, and God Himself proved — I repeat, my friends, *proved* — innocent. Where freedom is absolute and joy universal. In the words of God's promise to us through the lips of his anointed son Saint Peter Gilchrist,

' "If anything can go right, it will." '

Outside the west door, a beggar-child limps by, ragged and barefooted, her face smeared with dirt and tears.

1

Lord, Let Me in the Lifeboat

And the sun became black as sack-cloth of hair, and the moon became as blood; and the stars of heaven fell unto the earth . . . and the heaven departed as a scroll when it is rolled together.

——————— REVELATION 6:13-14 ———————

Edinburgh, Monday 20 August 2035

Black towers in the twilight. The clumsy stone daggers at their summits struggle to pierce the forenoon fog, struggle without success. The Scotch mist drifts and descends. For a moment all that is visible of Playfair's proud, sham, gothic building is the plaque at the foot of the steps:

> HOLOCAUST HOUSE.
> HOLY FEDERAL PARLIAMENT &
> ASSEMBLY OF THE KIRKS
> OF SCOTLAND. COLLEGE
> OF POST-NUCLEAR THEOLOGY.

As you mount the steps and penetrate into the courtyard, the statue of John Knox, preacher of fire and brimstone, obsessive foe of the monstrous regiment of women, strikes its demagogic pose above you. He is pitted, the old reprobate, with a century of grime and a month or two of gamma rays. The brimstone descended at last on him too, and his complexion is the worse for it. You pause and contemplate his face, having to tilt your head uncomfortably backwards so as to see it through the visor of your radiation-helmet.

3

A typical August day in twenty-first-century Scotland.

Half a mile away as the crow flies, Miss Jenny Blinkbonny was giving her catechism class to a restless group of teenagers. To be precise, thirteen thirteenagers, who had all reached the age of absolute boredom together, too listless even to raise their hands and create a diversion by demanding the loo. Except for one, a poor podgy lass with six fingers on both her hands who pipes up seriously:

'But why, why, miss?'

'Why *what*, Corinthia?'

Maureen Sutherland and Fiona Guthrie were giggling away behind their hands in the corner by the window: *Why is a mutant mute? Because she's a mute aunt.* In the opposite corner, two others were telling each other how magical and exworld the latest popstar is: 'He's intercontinental!' 'Mm, he's active!' this last being short, of course, for radioactive.

Corinthia MacAndrew has the prettiest of names — objectively, you had to admit that the sound of it rang like music off the tongue. Why Corinthia? Miss Blinkbonny wondered. Well, because it was one of those mythical places — forever mythical now, destroyed by the war of '98.

Why why is a good question, Miss Blinkbonny thought to herself. Aloud she said again, 'Why *what*, Corinthia?'

Corinthia, beetroot to the roots of her greenish mutant's hair, repeated her question doggedly: 'Why are we all sinners, Miss?'

'You must call me Miss Blinkbonny,' said Jenny automatically.

'Why are we all sinners, Miss Blinkbonny?'

'You must phrase your question more precisely, Corinthia. What makes you think we are not sinners? Do you think we are good to each other?'

Corinthia's blushes, she suddenly perceived, were due to indignation, not embarrassment. This girl really believed what she was saying, and was not merely trying to be difficult.

'Well,' said Corinthia, stating a truth too terrible for 13-year-olds to bear, 'my parents are good to me. And you, Miss Blinkbonny, you're good to me too. People really do try. Even those lassies in the corner there,' she said, turning to point at

4

Maureen and Fiona, whose tongues cleaved to their palates with fright as she did so, 'even those two lassies there, they don't really hate me. May I say something, Miss Blinkbonny, may I say something?'

'Of course, Corinthia.'

'I don't think deep down we feel wicked. Otherwise, why do we believe in God? *I don't believe in original sin.*'

Six-fingers, six-fingers, the girls muttered to each other, impressed despite themselves.

Jenny sniffed, sadly, not contemptuously. 'Well, Corinthia,' she said carefully, 'perhaps it's because of history. "History is crime," the Moderator says.'

'History, miss? You mean the *hollock*?'

The hol, the holoc, the holocaust. The class pricked up their ears. Silence, unusually, fell. Why are we here? What is the world about? What sort of creatures are human beings anyway? What monsters are our fathers and mothers who made us and the mutants, and who unmade so many others?

Oh dear, thought Jenny, what a question to be faced with when you are green and raw from teacher training, and you are only 21 and this is your first job and your first Monday morning catechism ever! What ought she to do? Try and steer them off into the Ten Commandments? But at least they were all sitting quiet and attentively for once. And after all, it was relevant, wasn't it?

Nothing more so.

Half a mile away again, in a huge glass and concrete shell that had once been Goldberg's Department Store, but was now a lovingly tended religious building, a thousand earnest and sober citizens were just reaching the climax of their worship. The Muslims have their Friday, the Jews their Sabbath, the Christians their Sunday, the Sacred Congregation of Christ the Destroyer has its Monday. For that was the day, thirty-seven years ago, when the Bomb dropped.

Both sexes were dressed for this ritual in boiler suits and protective shower-caps, and at this point there was an immense groaning and grinding of pews, loud whispers of 'Hush!' and

5

'Wheesht!' and a rustling of waterproof suiting as the congregation donned gloves, reached down to pick up the bags they had brought with them, then rose expectantly to their feet. Faces glanced eagerly about, lips murmured, the tide of emotion was mounting.

Even Peter Gilchrist was tugged for an instant out of his own grief. Yes, he thought, gazing around (for this was the first time he had attended such a ceremony), it's true what they say: that old lady in the next row, her lips are trembling. An audible sob came from the pews behind him: one of the women had tears pouring down her face.

'He is despiséd and rejected of men,' intoned the preacher.

'A man of sorrows and acquainted with grief,' chanted the congregation.

'And we hid our faces from him.'

'He is despised, and we esteem him not.'

'Surely he hath borne our griefs and carried our sorrows.'

Splat!

On the high wall behind the altar, arms out as if in the act of hovering, hung a crucifix with, attached to it, a beautifully faithful, man-sized copy of the image of Christ crucified in the Church of St Antony in Padua — though Padua, like Italy itself, no longer existed. What an expression of sorrow and dignity! The face half sunk towards one shoulder, inexpressibly weary, inexpressibly pitying of the poor tormented mortals that lifted their eyes towards Him.

Vlamm! Shruck! Two more bright red stains spattered the wall just above the halo. Gilchrist noted for the first time that this halo was curiously shaped. It was — surely not! — but yes, it was a mushroom cloud.

Squashed plums. The half-rotting fruit dripped, slithered down the wall, a few drops of rancid fruit juice splattered the God's naked shoulders.

'Yet we did esteem him stricken, smitten of God and afflicted.'

Thud! A rotten egg shattered hard against the crown of thorns. There was a loud sob of anguish from the fat, untidy mutant beside Gilchrist. It was from her hand that the egg had come.

'He is wounded for our transgressions ...'

6

Splew! Yash! Paroosh!

'... bruised for our iniquities.'

As one by one the congregation hurled their missiles, the image of Christ upon the wall began slowly to disappear behind an indescribable coating of filth — slime, rotting vegetable matter, putrefying flesh, bursting eggs, rancid fruit, refuse, scourings and scoriae.

Half the congregation were weeping now, tears pouring as they raised their arms and — Wham! Phutt! Shlaah! — mercilessly continued to pelt the suffering figure of Christ.

'The chastisement of our peace is upon him ...'

The foul covering of ordure on the body of Jesus glistened, slid, dripped and slavered onto the floor. Momentarily, His face with its fixed expression of suffering, of dignity, of compassionate love for humanity, reappeared, clean and quite unchanged, from behind the slithering filth.

'And with his stripes we are healed.'

Spladge! Thunk!

Gilchrist himself was still dry-eyed, though within him he was filled with all the grief of the past generation — the nuclear massacre, the peeling sickness, the years of plague, the sterility, the fear, the hopelessness. It all centred there, there on the image of God pinned by his outstretched palms to the wall.

And on it centred too all his own despair — the destruction of his own hopes, his own brief happiness.

'Well,' said Jenny, gazing round uneasily at thirteen pairs of blasé but critical eyes, 'where shall I start? You know about the War, I suppose.'

Some of her class nodded emphatically, others shook their heads with equal emphasis. Hands went up, and a babble of information was volunteered.

'We were bombed by the Russians, miss — '

'No we weren't, Christine, it was the English they nuked.'

'It was the whole *wurrld*, Fiona.'

'It was because our Moderator prayed for us that we got off so lightly,' said Aileen in self-righteous satisfaction.

'And then the red plague came ...'

7

'My dad says it was the Am, the Am, the Ammer-I-cans.'

Maureen Sutherland had difficulty saying the word because it was rather unfamiliar these days, almost as unfamiliar as the words Persepolis, Djibouti or Mohenjo-daro. After all, there weren't any Americans left either.

'You see, miss,' said Corinthia calmly from the front row, 'we don't get history until this year, not modern history that is. Miss, why *is* that? Why don't they tell us about the War?'

They're ashamed, Corinthia, thought Jenny to herself. Aloud she said, 'It's because it's supposed to be too horrible till you're old enough to take it.'

'Och miss, *do tell us*,' the girls chorused, licking their lips.

The young man with the white stick went tapping up the Mound as he did every morning, past the Academy and the National Gallery whose splendid Doric colonnades he could not see, still less the works of art that they contained (the sole surviving examples of El Greco, Rembrandt, Constable, and Van Gogh). Up the Mound he climbed, rapping at the railings to keep himself on course, knowing (though he had never seen it) that the Assembly Building, centre of government for the British Isles, what was left of them, was there standing silently above him. He raised his face towards it as he passed, just as he had every morning of his life. You could not say he raised his eyes, for he was born sightless.

When he was out in the open air, however, you could not see what form his blindness took, for he was covered from head to foot (like every other citizen of Scotland) in his radsuit, or oversuit, a kind of overall terminating in boots and topped by a shiny plastic helmet — a crude imitation of the clothing of a twentieth-century astronaut. Nonetheless, it was clear he was a blind man supported by the Commissioners of Charity, for the soiled and stained white of his oversuit proclaimed the fact.

One of the unlucky 12 per cent of our species of warmongers and mass murderers, a living and ever-present reminder of the evil that men do to one another.

'My grandmother,' Jenny was explaining, 'was one of the people who found herself standing on the bank when the first fugitives

8

came across the Solway Firth. Of course, people knew what had happened, but my grannie was a nurse and she was supposed to have a better idea what to do.

'The people in the boats were just sitting there, gazing ahead of them − it was shock, because they were burns victims mostly, and in pain.

'She told me she'd never forget what happened when the foremost boat touched the shore.

'She bent down to help the first person out. She was a pregnant girl, about 19 or 20, and grannie took hold of her by the hands, like this, you know − look Karen, let's do it the way she did it. You reach up, you see, and you put your hands out and I put mine out and we clasp each other's hands like that.

'Now, right, I haul you up.

'But it didn't happen that way with grannie. She gripped the young mother's hands in hers and pulled, but the skin of the girl's hands parted from her wrists and slid right off as if she'd been wearing gloves.'

'Ugh!' said the class as one girl, and Karen Mackenzie turned quite pale and sat down again at her desk, turning her hands this way and that and examining them.

'Has anyone here seen the "Carlisle Wall"?' asked Jenny.

Some looked mystified, but Susan put up her hand and said proudly: 'I have, miss, it's a great big red-stone wall that they brought all the way from the north of England and set up in the Kelvingrove Museum, and it's just like an ordinary wall only it has a kind of shadow on it, like the outline of a wee lad jumping in the air with a ball just two feet above his hands, that are reaching out, just about to catch it. You can see the shadow of the boy and the shadow of the ball too.'

'What a grand description, Susan. Do you know what it is?'

Susan looked immediately downcast, and shook her head.

'Well, when the megatons dropped on Carlisle, this wee boy was playing ball in the street. And when the Bomb drops, it sends out light so strong it's like being hit by a white-hot sledgehammer. So the wee lad's body, all his skin and bones and blood, were just vaporised − whew! − like a puff of smoke − and all that was left of him was his shadow burnt into the solid stone.'

9

The class was completely silent now, eyes big and round, and Karen was crossing herself.

'And then in the hospital — my grannie told me all this — the electricity had gone, so you couldn't see along the corridors. Worse, you couldn't do operations, because there was no light, no power, no water, and if there'd been water, how would it have been? Radiant.

'Besides, there were only ten beds in grannie's hospital for serious burns. Only ten, and as the day wore on, there were hundreds and thousands of poor folk struggling in from England.'

'Couldn't they ring for help?' said Christine Paterson.

'The telephones were out of order. You see, when a nuke goes zap in exspace, thirty miles high in the blue, it puts all the electronics out of kilter. No phones, no radios, no power in the electric plugs. It even wipes the tapes clean.'

'I don't see what's so sinful about us,' said Corinthia, irritatingly. 'Your grandmother helped, miss, and so did all the others. Does that not prove ... ?'

'Aye, aye, you can say that, Corinthia,' cried Aileen McInnes from the back of the class, 'but what about our own wicked fathers that put a touchlight to the whole bang-shoot?'

Gilchrist stumbled out of the Church of the Sacred Congregation of Christ the Destroyer, feeling bewildered, a wee bit relieved, a wee bit cleansed, a wee bit emptied of his pain.

The minister himself was on the steps of the kirk giving a fond greeting to his flock. Some of the filth had splattered his face, and he wore it proudly, for he was an intermediary between shepherd and indignant sheep.

Was it possible, if you went on throwing mud at the image of God, that one day He might notice? Gilchrist buckled up mentally on his own suffering, and at that moment his hand was grasped by the minister.

'A new face, I believe. Aye yes, I mind them all. And what would be your name, sir? I do hope you found the service ... *deeply* rewarding.'

This was Cairns Vajradatta Leitch himself, famous preacher, founder of the Church of Christ the Destroyer, member of the

Holy Federal Assembly, and the son of a worshipper of Kali and Yama, a quarter Tamil, it was said.

'Sir,' said Gilchrist, 'you invented this rite, I believe.'

'It is not my own, but God's. Nevertheless, I've found that people feel better for it.'

'In the old days there were only theists and atheists. Now there are antitheists too.'

'An oversimplification, sir,' said Leitch. 'The relationship between ourselves and our God is a complex one. You must come again and learn more of it.'

'I'm reminded of Shiva,' said Gilchrist cautiously.

'Aha, the dancer on the ruins,' agreed Leitch. 'The rites here, as you can guess, are something in the spirit of the Tantra . . . of the goddess Kali . . .' He was watching his subject narrowly to see if he were shocked.

'We have had the Apocalypse,' said Gilchrist, 'but the promised Second Coming is denied us.'

'That's not the question,' said Corinthia. 'I ken fine our fathers set a light to the rockets, aye, and made them too, but *who made our fathers*?'

The girls sniggered.

'It's a serious question,' said Jenny, intervening for once with real skill. 'Maybe our fathers and mothers were made out of a snigger as you, Sarah Mackintosh, suppose you were. But who made the world and everything in it?'

'God,' they chorused drearily.

'Who made the Devil, then, miss? God did too, didn't he, and then the Devil made Science.'

The lassies all made frightened faces at the word 'Science', and crossed their fingers for luck.

'And why did God make the Devil?'

The catechism went like clockwork, the logic of it swooping down as rapid as a bobsleigh till you came to the final absurdity.

'So as to tempt mankind.'

'So as to tempt us with what?'

The girls all giggled and whispered, and the catechism lost its route.

11

'Och miss, with *sex*,' said Susan, silver-eyed, round-mouthed.

The air split up like ice, jaggedly, as the girls giggled in disharmony, each to a different rhythm.

'But if God made the Devil, miss,' said Corinthia, 'and if he made us all able to hear him, then . . .'

'If God was to make us free, Corinthia, he had to give us the possibility of choosing between good and evil.' (Wasn't that the right argument, or something like it?)

Corinthia still looked unhappy. 'I'm not sure free will is a very good bargain, miss.'

Jenny looked startled, and asked why not.

'Well, so many people have had to die for the privilege of having free will. And they had to die so horribly. I can understand why *some* people should have to pay for us all to have free will. But why so *many*?'

Before Jenny had had time to recover from this, Susan Mears broke in, frowning in the way children have when they're sure there's an error in their thinking, and they want you, grown up and so entirely logical, to point it out to them. 'God is all-powerful, isn't he, miss?'

Jenny nodded automatically.

'So he must be free to prevent evil if he wants to.'

'Yes.'

'So why doesn't he, miss? If he can prevent evil and he doesn't, then he can't be all-good. And if he can't prevent evil, then he can't be all-powerful.'

Jenny was at a loss. This was David Hume's old argument, over two hundred years old, and how had this child, who had never heard of Hume, managed to reinvent it for herself? She suddenly saw that now, as a teacher employed by the Kirk, she needed more than faith. What she needed was fatherly advice from some dominie older and more experienced than herself. Not *too* much older. Just five years would do. She knew just the person. If only the bell would ring!

She was relieved when Fiona Guthrie put up her hand and asked how the Holocaust had started.

As Gilchrist retraced his steps along West Port, heading for his office on the Mound, the sights and sounds about him were all perfectly commonplace — a man on his knees in the middle of the street, praying in an anguished voice, oblivious of the passing horse-drawn traffic — a member of the Virtuous Mendicants with his begging bowl — a couple of flagellants (the only folk permitted not to wear the omnipresent radsuit) passing by with flails over their bruised and bloodied shoulders — and, as he entered the lower end of the Grassmarket, the usual handful of soapbox orators, each with a loudhailer pressed to the diaphragm of his radhelmet, each selling a different cure for the same universal disease — that of despair and of God's indifference.

This scene was too everyday to attract even the fringes of Gilchrist's attention. Shut behind the flaps of his oversuit, the shutters of his radhelmet, he felt as isolated as if he were in the desert. And suddenly all the anguish soothed and slaked away by the Rite of Desecration, came flooding back. He had not known that grief could present itself like a physical pain, like a cramp in the bowels, like the torments of harakiri. Doubled up with agony, he felt his way to a low wall at the foot of Castle Wynd and sat there clutching his stomach, gasping.

'Alison, Alison.'

The call from the hospital, the blow to the solar plexus.

Huddled on the low stone wall, but concealed from head to foot by his radsuit, Gilchrist looked like a robot whose machinery had seized up. The shiny leather-like surface of the suit, the glitter of the helmet put a barrier between him and the world. Though the suit was supposed to be a protection, it was really more of a prison. Even if one of the passers-by might have been moved to come up to him and offer some kind word or ask with concern what the matter was, to be locked away in his oversuit like this disguised what was wrong. He might have been sitting here thinking, quite happily. Or he might have been a down-and-out, of whom there were so many in the Grassmarket — always had been — except that his radsuit was so respectable-looking. Was this figure on the wall even male or female? It was an anonymous and separate world men lived in now!

Alison, his beautiful Alison, douce as a growing kitten, all

13

elbows and gestures and giggles . . . How delighted they had been when they learned the news! The figures were well known: two-thirds of all males, two-thirds of all females, sterilised by the terrible fall-out of '98 and '99, by the influx of rays from the stratosphere when the Bombs punched holes in the ozone layer, by all the slow but steady poison of the fall-out seeping back through their food and water ever since. So that only one in nine of all marriages was fertile — and the human race was not reproducing its numbers any more. Of course, there was P.E.S., the Partner Exchange System. Even so, they were not holding their own.

Alison and he had been among the lucky ones — and he had known at once it was going to be wonderful news when the doctor ushered them in personally, his face wreathed in smiles. 'Congratulations, Mrs Gilchrist, you're going to have a baby. It's not every day I have this happy duty . . .' There was genuine warmth in the doctor's voice.

And then, not four weeks later . . .

God had snapped his fingers again.

What was that old saying about 'not a sparrow falls . . .'? What irony! A cancer starts with a single nuclear collision — a particle is knocked out of a human cell. And then . . . the evil spreads, multiplies, swells up like a gobbet of foulness, annexes, subdues, invades the system. It starts with a single chance event.

An 'accelerated lethal carcinoma'. That, or something like it, had been the diagnosis.

Her life and the life of their child — snuffed out. Joy covered with a filthy scum, like the suffering face of Jesus on the Cross. Gilchrist felt he was choking. Careless of the most ordinary decencies, indifferent to what people might think, he tore at the fastenings of his helmet, and tugged it off.

Throughout the 1990s, Jenny was explaining to them, the governments of Western Europe had fallen one by one to the parties of disarmament. First in Italy, the *Unione per la Amicità Russa*; then in Germany, the *Sozialistischefreudefreiheitundfriedefederazion*, SF for short; then in Britain . . .

'Excuse me, miss,' said Karen, 'but what's Show — Show —

14

Show-salism? I ken fine it's a religion, but what *kind* of religion is it?'

When Jenny had defined it — it puzzled the girls, for politics was quite outside their experience — she went on to describe how Western Europe had thrown out the Americans, wrapped all its nukes in lead and concrete mantles and sunk them in caves in the middle of the Massif Central. Except for Britain, which was inefficient as ever, and months later had six nuclear submarines still harboured in the Holy Loch, simply because the bureaucracy hadn't 'implemented all the necessary processes'. And maybe 'Mad' Jimmy Renfrew, the admiral in command of the base, was dragging his feet.

How then one day in August '98, as the temperatures all over Europe soared into the nineties . . .

In Bonn, at three o'clock that afternoon, the Trotskyist—Pacifist government had lost a vote of confidence in the Bundestag. On television that night, the Chancellor, Doktor Gunther Fleisch, addressed the nation. His words deserve to be recorded verbatim.

'By the People of this Country we were, by the People to perform a Task, elected. Is the People's Will by the Treachery of a few renegade Deputies who all their Promises have forgotten, to be flouted? *Nein, nein, und nochmals nein.*'

Amid the chaos that followed his government's refusal to stop governing, he appealed to 'the friendly socialist States' to 'morally support' the German Volk. These socialist states complied with a batch of comradely tank divisions.

'But why,' asked Jenny, 'why stop at the Rhine? Particularly when there is nothing to stop you. Seven days after the incursion, the Americans had still done nothing, and doubtless the Russians thought they never would. For why should they defend someone else, when the result would be their own destruction?'

While the protests flew, all the sharp-nosed rockets pointed East and West, and the soldiers sat with their earphones on, fingers on the trigger, waiting for a Yes or a No.

And in China they thought how easy it would be to attack Russia and pretend it was the Yanks. And the Russians thought how easy it would be to attack China and pretend the same. And

15

all over the world, nations were gazing speculatively at their neighbours and having similar ideas.

Meanwhile, General Oblomov, who had advanced to the Marne 'for strategic reasons', declared that the USSR's purpose was a 'just revolutionary war to replace the outworn social systems of the West'. He called upon France and Britain to surrender, under pain of having Lyons and Birmingham 'taken out'. Doubtless the Russians were encouraged by the fact that on 11 August an earthquake centreing on New Madrid on the Mississippi, measuring 8·5 on the Richter scale, had devastated much of the central United States. The Yanks, they supposed, must have their minds elsewhere.

It is at such moments that politics resembles a game of chance, played around a table late at night by a handful of fanatics, whose wives have retired to bed in disgust — at the lack of conversation, the drunkenness of the players, the isolation of their senses from reality.

On 12 August, 'Mad' Jimmy Renfrew really did go mad. He issued a communiqué known later as the Declaration of Strone Point. Disarmament was, he declared, one final act of betrayal of the Scottish people by the mandarins of Whitehall. But he, he reminded them, still controlled a force of intercontinental ballistic missiles, and that force was now at sea somewhere in the Atlantic — or in the Baltic, or under the polar ice, who could say? He had instructed it to sail seven days ago, and he, Admiral Renfrew, hereby took charge of the defence of Scotland against Communist subversion, aggression, annexation, Socialist pacifism and southern English havering. Scotland at least would be defended against the crimson hordes from Asia. In the famous words which have come down to us, he stated:

'We Scots demand our birthright, which is the security and integrity of our nation. In pursuance of these vital interests, I hereby declare myself leader of the Provisional Government of Independent Scotland. Long live the Sacred Thistle and the Holy Loch.'

Four hundred miles away in London, the Cabinet wondered what to do. They had enough on their plate at the moment sending notes to the Russians, so they contented themselves with dispatching the Defence Minister, Herbert Barnes, to the Holy Loch to negotiate – thereby, as it turned out, saving Mr Barnes's life.

That was all they did and all they would ever do, for two days later – with the exception of Scotland, Tasmania, Lapland and some parts of the Sahara Desert – the whole world lay in ruins.

Renfrew had, by throwing his own eccentric, puzzling spanner into the Great Powers' doom-machine, saved Scotland's cities from the blast, the firestorm and the initial lethal pulse of radiation.

'Sir! Sir!'

There was a red radsuit bending over him in an attitude of concern. It was, he judged, a male voice speaking to him, though it was shrill with indignation, or perhaps embarrassment.

'Come now, sir, is this right and proper? Is it decent? This is no way for a respectable citizen . . . Bare-headed in full daylight! In the street! Really, sir.'

Gilchrist pulled himself together. 'I, I'm sorry,' he said hoarsely. 'I suddenly felt I was choking.'

'Choking?' said the red suit. 'More likely to choke with your helmet off!'

'And I had a pain here,' said Gilchrist, touching his stomach gingerly. The site of Alison's cancer. 'You must excuse me, I've had a terrible shock. My wife . . .'

'You need a s-s-stiff drink,' said the red suit more sympathetically, beginning to stutter as his embarrassment faded. He nodded as Gilchrist told the outline of his story. 'What do you say to the Deacon's Den? Just a step. Only you must put your helmet on again, *accelerando*. Here, let me give you a hand.'

'I'm supposed to be back at work in half an hour,' said Gilchrist weakly.

'Can't go in that state, c-c-c . . .' said the radsuit, sticking on the words 'can you?'

So the great century of materialism had gone down in blood like the sun, taking its materialism with it. In its place had arisen the twenty-first century, with its frantic sects, its occult lunacies, its guilt-ridden hatred of God.

But it remained a mystery why Scotland had been saved. Some uncertainty in the hand that should have pressed the button? A doubt on which side that obscure nation now stood? Ignorance as to where it actually was? The survival of Scotland was, to say the least, a miracle. To this day the Scots themselves could hardly believe it.

'Well, miss,' said Aileen McInnes, 'I think it proves we're nasty destructive animals. Deep down inside us, there's something badly wrong. My mum says that and she's the Head and she should know.'

'Aye, but who made us that way?' objected Corinthia. 'I'll tell you who it was. God.

'And besides, miss, miss,' she added in great excitement, 'that last detail you told us, about how when the Bomb had dropped and half the population of the world was dead and the sun near blotted out for a month and the crops were dying and the people too and all the radiation . . . how a mysterious new disease came just out of nowhere, and finished what the nukes had begun. Just when we could all have done with a miracle too!' she added triumphantly.

'Aye, well maybe you're right, Corinthia,' said Fiona. 'It was a miracle all right, a black miracle.'

'But God saved Scotland from it!' protested Aileen.

'No, he didn't,' retorted Susan scornfully, 'it was the doctors. We had the only hospitals still standing, and they sat down and worked out an antidote, just in time. It was Iain Bruce Davidson that did it, 'cos my father's told me about it.' For Susan Mears was a doctor's daughter.

Corinthia turned back to Jenny, passionately. 'What do *you* think, Miss Blinkbonny? Is it not an evil, evil world? I'm not surprised God never shows his face in it, he's too ashamed and that's for sure.'

'Aye, miss,' breathed Susan, scared by her own temerity. 'It's not we that are the sinners, it's God.'

Aileen drew her breath in sharply at the blasphemy.

18

West Bow still looked much as it had fifty years before, in the 1980s, for since the cities had been flattened, modern man had had a superstitious horror of destroying buildings. There was a difference in the people, however, for they were all concealed from head to foot in oversuits, shapeless and anonymous, or nearly so. It took a keen eye to recognise even a close friend under such a garb. Gilchrist had often wondered why, nearly forty years after the Holocaust, folk still wore it. The fall-out had long since stabilised, and in any case the radsuit was not airtight, had no longer any practical utility at all, but was purely symbolic.

And why were most radsuits black?

The monstrous deformities of 12 per cent of the population were thereby kept decently hidden from the eye. But the main reason was that mankind's cheerful, outgoing confidence had given way to an introverted fearfulness, a dread of the very world that supported their lives. For the same reason, the odd twentieth-century custom of sunbathing was now unknown, and children who came across the habit in history books were amazed and uncomprehending. What, expose your skin to the open air? Unthinkable. What was a suntan but radiation burns?

As Gilchrist and his new acquaintance climbed the steep curve of West Bow, therefore, nothing of interest offered itself to the eye but the notices in the windows advertising one church or another − a plethora of cults − the Covenant of the Holy Wafer, the Clapping Hand of Zen, the Church of Christ Pacifist, Sri Mahalinka's School of Meditation, the Galloway Druids, the Divine Astronauts, the Christian Feminists (who called Arthur's Seat 'Martha's Seat') − along with the remnants of much older faiths, the Wee Frees, the Piskies (or Episcopalians), Jehovah's Witnesses and the three modern varieties of Papism. Then there were the groups with the puzzling names − well, you wondered what in heaven their doctrines could be − the Friars Forgetful, the Church of Extravagant Promises, the Temple of Little Faith . . .

They stepped into the roadway to avoid a couple of Huxleyites sprawled in a psychedelic stupor across the pavement, and climbed on up the hill and round the corner, where there beckoned Deacon Brodie's Inn, dedicated to the memory of that respectable businessman, burglar and cut-throat, the original

Jekyll and Hyde. The stink of warm beer wafted out of its open door, sickly as a drunkard's breath.

'Why, hello, Jenny,' said Alec Jamieson, lifting his head from the mark-books on his desk and smiling. For one thing it was a joy to the eyes to look at her. For another thing he had been going to catch her at the end of the morning's lessons, strike up a conversation, invite her for lunch, see where it all led. A hopeful sign, he thought to himself, her coming to me first. He noted, however, the slight cloud of worry in her eyes, the slight pout of her lips that, truth to tell, made them still more attractive.

'You're looking every so slightly worried,' he said. 'Did the catechism go right?'

'Och . . . yes . . . well, not too badly, I think, but . . . Alec, if I'm not too much of a bore, I'd dearly love some advice. I don't somehow fancy talking to the Head about it, you know.' She faltered to a silence.

Such a pretty girl, and looking to me for advice! cried Alec inwardly. Aloud he said, 'Jenny, what ever can you mean? How could any man in his right mind be bored talking to *you*? As to Mrs McInnes, I don't blame you, she's an ostrich of a woman, her head aye in the sand and that sand's called the One True Kirk of God.'

'Aye, but her daughter's in my class,' said Jenny with a sinking heart. 'Heaven knows what she'll tell her mother!'

'I tell you what,' said Alec, 'when you've taught your next one and I've run out of red ink, why don't you come to lunch with me and we'll talk it all over? How would the Deacon's Den suit you?'

Down on the ground floor of Deacon Brodie's, the young man in the white suit removed his radhelmet, placed it neatly on the seat beside him, put down his white stick, reached for the pint of heavy with the practised accuracy of a sighted man. He felt a slight rustle on the seat beside him and turned his face full in that direction. His neighbour gazed with shock at this mask that was presented to him — a face and skull quite hairless, the shape of a naked human buttock, or like a blank white sheet of parchment on which some artist had painted in merely two things: a pair of eyebrows and a pair of bright red lips. A surrealist face, a joke in very bad taste, for the artist had left out the eyes, so that the skin of the cheeks rose without interruption to meet the eyebrows, and a visage as smooth and sightless as a chamber-pot faced him. The man made a move as if to get up and change seats, but the blind man reached forward and grasped him by the sleeve.

'Have we met, friend? I cannae see your face, ye ken.'

'John Maclain,' replied the other weakly.

'Good day to you, John Maclain,' said the blind man, not releasing his grip. He leaned forward confidentially. 'I'll no tell you my name, for I'm here incognito. You see, I'm the Risen Christ.'

2

Really the Blues

The hungry sheep look up,
and are not fed.

———————— MILTON ————————

Outside the pub door, the blue suit and the red, Gilchrist and his rescuer, paused and discussed the serious question of a drink. Duty called Gilchrist to his office, grief and his new acquaintance drew him towards the consolations of ever so slightly radioactive whisky. Seen from the opposite pavement of the High Street, their movements, their gestures, seemed not quite in phase with each other. It was as if they were acting in two different productions of the same play.

The blue suit pointed down the Mound, the red one towards the open door, nodded 'Just as you please', then shook Gilchrist's hand before stepping, alone, into the tavern. Gilchrist turned the corner and hurried on down the Mound towards the nine-storey building that is Redemption House, home of the Kirk of Scotland Publications.

Or perhaps not. Perhaps he weakened, decided to let the office slide for an hour or so. His habits were too automatic to defend themselves against his grief. Perhaps that was what happened, so that the slow pavane of red and blue suits moved to a slightly different choreography, and culminated in their both stepping through the tavern door.

Inside, they cast an eye around. This ground floor bar was all polished Victorian oak and shining mirrors, in which the scene was reproduced several times from various angles, as if each reflected version were a subtly discordant reality. A circle of working men, some sitting, some standing as if turned to stone at different haphazard moments, like birds hypnotised by a snake. All were listening in silence to a white-suited youth, bald and eyeless, like an egg with a mouth, who was whispering rather than speaking. The red suit and the blue removed their helmets so as to read the message in each other's eyes, then without a word moved on towards the upstairs bar.

There both unzipped their overclothes and revealed beneath them a pair of suits, subfusc, the old twentieth-century cut that breathed a safe pre-nuclear respectability. For despite the fact that the windows were open on the High Street beyond, this room was technically 'indoors'.

'Peter Gilchrist.'

All Gilchrist received in response to this was a mumble of sounds to which he could attribute no sense.

'I beg your pardon?'

His rescuer made a great effort and pronounced the words: 'Virgil Appelbaum. I'm of American origin, you s-s-see.'

'Of course,' said Gilchrist. He meant it to sound polite but, as he sat down, thought it must seem downright rude.

His new acquaintance was like many shy people, quite impervious to rudeness. He began to explain that he was 30 years old, that his parents had been part of the American exodus — the new 'P-p-pilgrim Fathers' who had landed on the west coast of Scotland in the autumn of '98.

'Believers in Atlantis, UFOs, Sigmund Freud, the land of Mu, the Hobbits . . .'

'Moo?'

'*Rallentando*, you must let me explain.' Virgil waved his hands and giggled.

Gilchrist gazed at him, interest in this strange individual lifting him for a moment out of the well of self-pity in which he was drowning. Though Virgil claimed to be 30, and the absence of lines on his face seemed to bear this out, he was somewhat bald, his hair growing in patches, each tuft fluffy and flying off in a contrary direction like a burning — or perhaps bursting — bush. When he spoke, he jerked his arms about, spluttered, stuttered, as if he existed at the same time in several not quite simultaneous realities, and as if one could hear the start of the same sentence constantly overlapping itself. He *shimmered*. He was like a photograph on which several exposures had been taken.

23

'So I was brought up a member of the Cult of Von Däniken,' concluded Virgil.

'The Chariots of the Gods? The people who think the world was founded by little green men?' said Gilchrist incredulously.

'*Pianissimo!*' begged Virgil with a pizzicato giggle. He looked nervously around. 'I work for them. I'm in the publicity department.'

They sat over glasses of whisky the colour and flavour of the northern peat-streams, and Gilchrist, pressed, told his story, finding it comforting to do so, even to a stranger. All he wanted was an ear, all he wanted was to empty himself. He was a broken dam with words spilling out of it.

After a while an older man in his late thirties came in, signed to Virgil and sat down with an air of indifference, almost as if he were not listening. As Gilchrist's tale continued, he nodded his head like someone going through the motions of concern. Finally, as impassive as ever, he beckoned the waitress and bought them all another round.

'This is my boss,' stammered Virgil. 'Archie McDonald Rimmon, publicity chief of Von Däniken's.'

'A descendant of the MacRimmons,' the new arrival announced, and held out his hand to be shaken. You imagined on first seeing him that he must have difficulty in speaking, because his mouth was so tightly connected at the corners, leaving only a small horizontal slit through which the words could sidle. A puritan mouth, an opinionated mouth, a secretive mouth. 'Sorry to hear of your troubles,' he added calmly. 'Perhaps my Kirk can help.'

He permitted a brief burst of laughter to escape him, then leaned forward: 'To tell the truth, I've always wanted to invent a new religion, only I'd need a prophet, a martyr — preferably one and the same person — a doctrine ...'

Gilchrist wondered whether Rimmon's cynicism was real or affected.

Meanwhile, Alec Jamieson and Jenny Blinkbonny were advancing up George IV Bridge towards the same pub, talking as they went. This was easier than might appear, for a button in the mouthpiece switched on a small amplifier which enabled you to be heard. It was rather like talking to someone on the telephone, and normally it was hard to convey any human feeling. But for once, today, as they walked on past Bobby's Bar and Soutar's Bookshop, the enveloping plastic helmet was no obstacle, and the young people found themselves chatting in the easiest and friendliest of fashions. Really, it was all going swimmingly. Jenny had already broached the problem of her catechism class, and been consoled by Alec who told her firmly (and sincerely) that she had handled it, aye, in the best possible way.

'Children *thinking*? Asking *questions*? Jenny, you're a born teacher!'

'But Mrs McInnes.'

'Don't you worry your pretty head about her. What was wee Corinthia preaching this morning but the doctrine of Christ the Destroyer? It can't be a heresy if 5 per cent of the population believe it, and that's official. The federal constitution of the Kirks proclaims it!'

Jenny looked thoroughly grateful. A load was lifted from her mind. 'To tell the truth – it's a terrible thing to admit, but I think the thing that put me off balance this morning wasn't so much Aileen McInnes and her surplice-faced mother, but – well, Alec, do *you* ever have doubts? Do *you* wonder if the Kirk is right?'

How good my name sounds on her lips, thought Alec, and how refreshing it is not to have superstitious nonsense about science rammed down one's throat, as it is by some up-to-date young women.

'How dreadful it would be,' she went on, 'if Corinthia were right, and there were no God. What would folk do? Who would they call upon in time of need? Wouldn't they lose heart and . . .'

'What makes you think we've any heart to lose? Pretty demoralised already, aren't we? Why are we all still in Scotland, can you tell me that, thirled to our own wee nation like frightened sailors clinging to a raft? The radiation levels fall and fall by the year, yet Europe's still as empty as the moon, just as it has been these last thirty years. Why haven't we gone out again to colonise the world like the Elizabethans, like the Scots in the nineteenth century? Instead of which the human race has had all the stuffing

25

knocked out of it. Guilt and fear, remorse and cowardice. Do you know, I even sometimes wonder if fertility . . .'

They were cutting off each other's sentences now as if they had known each other for years. 'Och, I've wondered that myself. But isn't the reason this? When the Bomb fell, folk lost their faith in God.'

The suicide rate, forty times higher than it had been before the Bomb. The infanticide of deformed children. The mutants huddled in their ghettos at Leith, Bonnyrigg and Pilton.

'Well, you know, Jenny, there wasn't much faith around in the twentieth century. Politics was the thing in those days, science and similar superstitions. It took the Bomb to scare the living daylights out of us all and turn us back into wee church mice.'

To himself he thought: How charmingly natural the word 'faith' sounds on her lips!

As they reached the crossroads at the northern end of George IV Bridge, Jenny looked around and wondered, Shall I? Och, why not?

'Is it Deacon Brodie's you really want to go to, Alec? Why not the Jolly Judge? I like it there.'

'O.K.,' he says.

O.K., he says, *if* she says that. But she doesn't say it, because she's a traditionally brought up lass, and equality died with the Bomb in '98, and nice young ladies like to seem demure and not too forthcoming — at least for the first few meetings. So she didn't say any such thing and in consequence they walked right across the High Street, in at the side door of Deacon Brodie's, and up the stairs to the first floor. There three men whose acquaintance they hadn't yet made were already ensconced over a glass of Highland Malt.

The two young people were served, and turning from the buffet table, hesitated, scanning the packed and noisy room. Not a seat to be seen, but as they glanced at each other and took a second look around the pub with its neat red and white checked tablecloths, its little shaded lights, its windows opening on the chilly mist of the High Street, a couple by the window got up . . .

Or perhaps not. No, in fact it was a couple of women who rose from the other two chairs at Gilchrist's table. 'You can have our

26

seats, we're just away.' They took their radsuits down from the peg and climbed with practised smoothness into them, their deformed mutant shapes disappearing behind the modest bulkiness of helmet and overall. Alec and Jenny sat gratefully down. They were too interested in each other to take notice of the three older men at the same table.

'Dungeons and Dragons,' Rimmon was saying. 'Tunnels and Trolls, Arcturans and Astronauts. Mad on these fantasy games, my two are.'

He has children, thought Gilchrist, feeling that the packed inn around him was a desert of loneliness.

'Eighteen and 17, you'd think they'd have grown out of all that. Can't face reality, the young, these days. Like the whole science-damned world.'

'Science-damned' was an expletive only slightly less popular than 'White Blood'. Besides, it was two oaths for the price of one. Gilchrist winced. He had been taking an interest in the occult lately — the forbidden sorcery of quantum physics. It wouldn't do, though, to hint of that to strangers.

'That's a game of alternative choices, isn't it?' said Virgil. 'Every turn you take, you have a decision. Whether to ring the bell, or knock, or b-b-break down the door *fortissimo*.'

'Might-be's and might-have-been's,' said Gilchrist. 'Have you ever thought, "Why am I here? Why, in all the possible worlds that might have been, do I find myself in *this* one, this strange Scotland of the twenty-first century which by some fluke has survived alone, where England to the south of us is a wilderness full of insects, empty wind and grass, and the whole continent of Europe is inhabited by a few hill-farmers?" Why should *we* have survived? What have we done to deserve that?'

The couple beside them had still not emerged from the interest of their own conversation. Despite the fact they sat at the same table, there was no reason why Gilchrist and Rimmon, Alec and Jenny should ever exchange a word.

'No, I haven't,' said Rimmon, but Gilchrist was beginning to recognise that the man's tone of indifference was a permanent trait.

He went on: 'Come to that, why am *I* here? Why are *you*?

27

Doesn't it all rest upon the most extraordinary chances? My father used to tell me of a day back in '03 — he had supplies to deliver to Cumbernauld — drugs and serums. Well, the van broke down, and he had to stay kicking his heels in town another night. Since he had time to spare and nothing to fill it with, the landlady asked him if he'd deliver a message for her to a street half a mile away. My father agreed and duly set off, pausing in his walk after a while to ask the way. Finally he arrived at the right door and knocked. It was opened by an old lady who told him, "No, sir, there's nobody of that name here. Och," she added, looking at the address on the letter my father was holding, "you're come to the wrong street. This is Kilkenny Street and not Kirkcaldy Street." And she gave him the right directions. My father set off again, but, as he was only halfway down the road, the heavens opened in a real Glaswegian cloudburst which would have soaked my father to the skin, right through his radsuit, if he hadn't taken refuge in the nearest common stair.'

'I follow you,' said Rimmon. 'It was "Russian rain" back in '03, wasn't it? Radioactive death. Science-damned rain.' He gave out a gasping bark, like a poor actor pretending to laugh.

'Well, as he stood there in the hall with the door half open, watching for the downpour to stop, a young lass slipped into the doorway beside him. It turned out she lived on the same street and had just missed her bus because she'd found she didn't have her purse in her handbag. Och, they began talking, and ...'

'Let me guess,' said Rimmon. 'That was how your father met your mother. So that, if it hadn't been for the van breaking down and the misdirection by the man in the street, and the sudden shower of Russian rain, and your mother forgetting her money ...' But he did not seem to be amazed, like Gilchrist, at this shocking tangle of coincidences.

There was a silence, and a snatch of the conversation between the young couple came drifting across the table.

'So there I was,' Alec was saying, 'sitting in the electrobus, and I could see these two old wives cracking away in front of me. "I always find the launderette so convenient," says the first.

' "Aye," says the other, "it's such a blessing having your own washing machine."

28

' "That's true," says the first, "it's gey friendly in the launderette, you can chat away while you're waiting."

' "Just my opinion," says the second, "you can get on with naebody to bother you."

'Now what on earth was going on? Did they really not know they were disagreeing with each other?"

'In two different worlds,' said Jenny with a little snort of laughter. She began to tell a story in her turn, and Gilchrist glanced mournfully across at her, taking in almost despite himself, the pretty picture that she made.

Her movements were jerky, expressing liveliness. There was an excited flush on the tips of her cheekbones. As she talked her head nodded and shook in time to her statements, emphasising the end of each sentence. Her poise was tense, her legs crossed, her body leaning forward as if she were about to rise energetically and cast her glass into the far corner. Her eyes were a vivid pale blue, sparkling as she moved her head. Her mouth was pink and mobile, dedicated to the rapid production of words. The free hand (the one not holding a glass) flexed from the wrist as it danced, asserted and deprecated in rhythm to her meanings.

This girl was dark, and Alison had been a sunny blonde. This one had high Celtic cheekbones, and his Alison had had a rather long and slender face. But their mannerisms were similar — the same angular energy, the same rapidity of chatter.

Gilchrist had a sinking feeling. Why am I here? The chance of the carcinoma, wasn't it the same thing exactly? Countless millions to one, but that one is yourself, conscious, viewing the bright, round, beautiful world with naïve and thoughtless hope. God's roulette table spins. Countless millions to one, but this time your number is up: an electron jumps out of its orbit, the chain of causality flicks into motion, a cell inflates into a devouring monster, a woman dies.

'Why am I here?' said Gilchrist again. 'And how I wish I wasn't!'

He stretched out his hand and plucked Rimmon by the sleeve, blaming God:

'Why does it have to be like this? The effect following the cause, regular as clockwork? It isn't as simple as people think. You aim your stick at the tree, and an apple falls. You clap your hands and the fly buzzing round your head falls dead on the grass. Only it isn't like that, is it? Why, you can perfectly well aim and miss, and folk do, all the time. There's plenty of room for chance, you must agree. And that being so, there's plenty of room for God. He could intervene as much as he likes, *and no one would ever notice.*

'Only he doesn't, does he? He didn't in '98, or with Alison yesterday.'

For the first time tears sprang to his eyes. He began to sob openly, an ugly, shameful sound, putting his head down on the table in total surrender, so that his full glass of whisky splashed and smashed onto the floor beside his feet.

Jenny, beside him, was caught quite speechless in the midst of her sentence. Her right hand took on a will of its own: she could feel it wanting to stretch out and pat the dark hair at the crown of Gilchrist's head.

Rimmon sat stock-still as if waiting for something entirely different to happen. Virgil pressed his hands together, then felt for his mouth, meanwhile glancing around the pub in embarrassment. *Con amore*, he thought, then, several seconds later, blushed.

'What is the matter?' said Jenny in concern, across the top of Gilchrist's head. Rimmon explained, frowning slightly, as if to show sympathy — though purely out of a sense of decency. The man's wife ... they'd been going to have a child ... a tragedy ... you mustn't take any notice of his blaming God ... grief has upset his religious balance ... luckily he has friends here ...

From the table came the terrible tearing sounds of human pain. Gilchrist himself felt frightened by his tears, as if it were blood streaming from his eyes.

'What ever are we going to do?' said Jenny. 'We can't just leave him alone like this. We must telephone his employer and say he can't possibly come in this afternoon. Do you know where he stays? Maybe someone should sit with him for a while ...'

Alec, who had been taking a back seat during this discussion, touched Jenny's hand. 'Perhaps we shouldn't interfere. I know it's a school half day this afternoon, but Mr Rimmon here is evidently a good friend, and ...'

This only made matters worse. Alec had spoken out of a dim

and unspecifiable sense of disquiet, but to do so at all was a false step.

Jenny turned to him firmly. 'No. Alec, if folks don't make themselves *responsible*...'

During the last few exchanges, Rimmon had risen to his feet, imperiously demanding another whisky for his friend. At the same time he had whispered to the others that he really had to be away, since duty called. Gilchrist was in good hands, and ...

Meanwhile, a small blonde radsuit had entered, its creases suggesting that the person within was plump in detail but exquisitely petite *in toto*. Unzipping like a honeydew melon, the small blonde radsuit split open to reveal a small blonde lassie, round of face with a wide pink mouth, who advanced towards their table crying — 'Jenny! Fancy seeing *you* here!'

'Och, Helen,' murmured Jenny, her mind elsewhere.

Rimmon, having vacated the chair he was about to leave, offered it to the new arrival.

Then he looked round for another, and sat down again.

3
Always, All Alone and Stumbling

They go to the cliffs of Moher
rising out of the mist,
Above the real,
Rising out of present time and
place, above
The wet, green grass.

——————— WALLACE STEVENS ———————

Edinburgh, Saturday 29 September 2035

Under Jenny's insistence, Gilchrist had stayed off the bottle for the last fortnight and out of the pub. His appearances at the publisher's office had become punctual again, he had resumed regular meals, and this afternoon he had even begun to shuffle through the manuscript of the book he had been working on before Alison's death. He found, however, that he could not keep his mind on the text, and was that really so surprising? The occult works of twentieth-century physics — Planck's constant, Heisenberg's principle of uncertainty, the Einstein–Rosen–Podolsky paradox — had taken on the strangeness of some Bavarian folly, hypergothic, absurd — or like Magritte's *Pyrenean Castle*, an impossible object floating unsupported in an empty sky. Twentieth-century thought! It was plainly the ravings of a lunatic imagination!

Besides, faces and images would keep intervening between him and the page — Jenny frowning at him worriedly, Alison giggling, opening her arms to him... The spectres of guilt emerged again from the darkness where they always lurked. Though he knew fine well that he was blameless, he found himself whispering, 'It's my fault, my fault,' in an agony of self-

32

reproach; and his cosy sitting room, with its comfortable chairs, its bookcases, its pale blue curtains, seemed as grim as a prison cell where he sat awaiting trial for the murder of his wife. Raising his eyes to the mirror on the chimney-breast, a curious illusion imposed itself: through the wall was to be found, not the familiar kitchen of his flat, but an identical replica of the room where he was sitting, and Alison was there, laughing and talking as she sipped her tea, and he was there too, another Gilchrist, an alternative version of himself — as if the reality we inhabit is not the sole reality, but merely one of a range of variant worlds. But here he was, trapped inside the here and now, and no man knew how to quit the reality he dwelt in and step through the mirror into that other world where Alison, perhaps, was still alive, and the baby too.

He could almost hear her voice, raised in laughter as she recited her day to him, could almost hear the answering words of his other self.

He rubbed his eyes and pushed the battered manuscript aside. He turned to the magnetograph, for music perhaps . . .

One of those things from the 1945 sessions, three minutes long, ninety years old. *Minor Swoon.* Pure improvised joy, with the trumpeter, Page, cutting out a tune as rough edged as a jigsaw, Mezz Mezzrow squeaking away like a badly oiled gate, and then Bechet the great man himself coming in on the soprano for the last two choruses, majestic, riding over them all like God's salvation, like the sun coming out. The old Creole from New Orleans, with his half-delinquent ways, his face as brown and battered, his head as bald, as a Zulu knobkerry, his body long mouldered away into the red French soil of Garches, but his music sounding out into the air of Gilchrist's flat as it had nearly a century ago in that New York studio. Three minutes of rescued time, fresh and as if new minted. You could hear harsh excitement in the vibrato, as the old man made it new yet again — 'The music has to let you be . . . You gotta stay free inside it.'

Precious archives of a vanished music, but even they provided no relief this evening. Indeed, they reminded him of other losses too, for he had inherited them from his father. Perhaps a walk on the mountain to clear his head . . .

Outside in the street, at the foot of the common stair, a group of small boys were improvising too, whooping and yelling, playing space-raiders, firing off toy automatics. Television was part of the forbidden technology, the adult world had gone resolutely pacifist, so where had they learned such behaviour? Original sin, the Kirk would say, and maybe they were right for once, for the nature of small boys remained determinedly itself no matter how the teaching of their parents changed.

He set off down Rankeillor Street, forcing himself to step briskly, heading for the mountain.

Arthur's Seat is almost the smallest mountain ever called by that name, being only eight hundred feet high (not 250 metres, for the old measures had been reintroduced, out of disgust for everything the twentieth century had found 'up to date'). It is an easy climb, a mere gentle evening stroll to the top and, as you ascend between iron-black outcrops of rock and unkempt tangles of gorse, the horizon expands around you, revealing first the whole vista of the city, with the shores of the Firth of Forth running along its northern fringe, then the Forth upstream to Queensferry where the two bridges used to stand (they collapsed in '08 at the height of the post-nuclear confusion, and are now tangled heaps of rusting iron, like the wreckage of old battleships). Then, as you reach the summit with its torn volcanic rocks, once jagged, now polished smooth by a million footsteps, the northern horizon fills with distant mountains — the whole sweep from Ben Lomond in the west to the more rounded waves and billows of the Grampians. Gilchrist stood at the top, the wind chilling him, taking pleasure in the beauty of the sight, standing a little apart from the half dozen other citizens who were already admiring the view. He particularly averted his eyes from a couple with their arms around each other, and after a moment went off a little distance to survey the line of the Old Town below him. Edinburgh's first presence had begun upon this spine of hillside, that was still clearly marked out by a line of towers and spires — the Castle, the Camera Obscura, the Tolbooth Kirk, St Giles, the Tron ... and so on down to the Palace of Holyrood at the foot of the mile-long slope.

The centre of Edinburgh was still intact. It was the further outskirts that were missing, all those suburbs and high rise flats that had been built in the great expansion of the previous century. Now that the population had shrunk to a mere hundred thousand, there was no need of that vast spread. The houses had crumbled, the wilderness had invaded, the city was surrounded by a rim of decayed and perilous ruins, mounds of rubble half concealed by brambles and hogweed, empty roofless houses with trees bursting through their walls. The science buildings of the University, a mile south from the centre, had been abandoned, for the Science Faculty, greatly reduced in numbers and renamed the Technology Institute, had withdrawn to the inner city. All that was left of the Maxwell Building was its metal framework, still rearing into the sky but rusted and twisted, as skeletal as a fossil brontosaurus and twice as dead.

Gloomy, meditative, he turned his back on the deserted suburbs, and settled himself on the grass at the northern corner of the summit, gazing over at the 'Kingdom' of Fife on the opposite shore of the Forth. As he sat there, his consciousness caught in a trough of vacancy midway between his sorrow and the beauty of the scene, the evening luminosity spread gradually from sky to sea, till he could no longer distinguish where the one ended and the other began. A deceptive, mesmeric light, so both sea and sky blended like a single silver cloth, glowing from within, hung vertically between zenith and nadir, upon which a play of silhouettes and shadows is enacted. The Forth, its long arm full of white space, seemed part of the air, a deep cleft of luminous emptiness undercutting the dark shores of Fife, which hung unsupported, a black cloud upon the face of the sky-sea. Gilchrist felt a sense of vertigo, for it was as if the curve of the globe had contracted like a clenching fist, and the horizon lay now at his feet, at the edge of the estuary's strand below him. Above it, the land mass of Fife floated impossibly in space.

The illusion flicked back again into its previous, equally perturbing form, and again he saw sea and sky as a huge white cloth held up before his eyes, a screen behind which some other, different reality lay concealed.

He held his breath, as for some revelation. Behind the screen of light, behind what Indians call the Veil of Maya, what other reality

35

lay in wait? It was as if the land were about to lift off sky and sea like a child's transfer. But nothing happened, only the chill gusting of the wind, and the light darkening on sea and sky as every moment passed.

He was thirsty after his climb, but to think of that was not a good idea.

A faint chanting began to be audible at the foot of the slope, and glancing in that direction he could see the flicker of lanterns like an approaching galaxy of stars. In the year 2000, a desperate ragtag of people, many of them on the point of death, had climbed to the top of Arthur's Seat, expecting to ascend into heaven. Disappointed, some had adopted the only known method of achieving such an ascent, namely throwing themselves off the edge of the Crags. Others, however, (whose faith was either stronger or weaker, depending how you looked at it) had reminded themselves that the date of Christ's birth was uncertain. It might be worthwhile returning in a year's time. And so, the years had passed, the time appointed for the mass ascension of the Faithful had been postponed and then postponed again, till it had begun to coincide with the date of the crucifixion. The Kirk of the Shining Morn (said their opponents) always expected Christ's return *tomorrow*.

And here they were again, hastening up the slope with their latest and most up-to-date prediction, hoping that tonight it really would be the end at last!

It was not his fault, he told himself. He had been hounded away. At his feet the grass was still that eerie green which you see in late evening, in autumn, as the sun sinks lingeringly, doubtfully, behind the western mountains. A terrain of falling spaces, of loose shale, rabbit holes, delusions and shadows. He began to pick his way carefully back down the mountainside, intending to take the shortest route home.

As he descended into the darker gloom of the valley, passed the old bonded warehouse and entered the first street, his own feelings too became darker, as if these grey and dusty thoroughfares, where pieces of rubbish blew in the night wind, were the bric-à-brac of his own mind. His flat would be inhuman, littered with silent books and empty shadows which a woman once had animated. The only escape offered was that lighted doorway through which there wafted scraps of conversation and whiffs of beer-laden air. He owed himself the luxury of surrender − to human company and to his guilt.

'Just one,' he said, and then was aware he had said it aloud.

The bar glowed with light and a pretence of warmth. It was human but impersonal, as such places are. It was just what he needed, for it offered neither kind of reality − the desert nor friendship.

At the bar, he surveyed the row of beertaps, wondering aloud, 'Which one shall I have?'

The barman, evidently a humorist, replied. 'Tell me how much you've got and I'll tell you what you can have.'

Gilchrist at once felt huddled away in the warm anonymity of bar conversation, generalities and jokes with folk you had never met before and would never meet again, that vague expansive warmth towards humanity that is standardised and therefore safe.

But there was more to it than that. When he drank, his irrational feeling of guilt and his hatred of God both grew. They grew to the point where they eliminated each other, like two waves which, expanding far enough, 'interfere' and are mutually abolished. He would reach a sort of peace, and at closing time would escape to his flat and cast himself fully clothed upon the blankets with a buzzing in his ears and the bed keeling like a boat.

When Jenny found him, two hours later, and doucely complained that his resolution had lasted but two weeks, he protested, 'I like these people. I can talk to them.'

'You can talk to me,' said Jenny.

4

I Told You Once,
I Told You Twice

Pilate saith unto Him,
What is Truth?

————— JOHN 18:38 —————

Friday 8 February 2036

'Mr Gilchrist,' said the Chairman, 'we have called you here this
afternoon before a full meeting of the Publications Board, to
which we have invited the Moderator himself, for he has a special
interest in one of the matters we shall be discussing. I have to tell
you, sadly, that we have come to our provisional decision, and
there is little likelihood of any alteration in it. However, we do not
wish our proceedings to be a reproach unto us in the eyes of men,
and have called you here so that you may have the opportunity to
defend yourself. I shall ask the Moderator to speak in due course,
but in the first instance . . .'

Inside the Boardroom of Redemption House, everything was
black leather, glossy mahogany, deep pile carpets. Behind the
chairman's seat (occupied this afternoon by their eminent
visitor, the Moderator himself) there hung a simple wooden
cross, from which the figure of Christ was absent. On the left-
hand wall were portraits of past chairmen, all darkly robed and
most with grey, inquisitive faces. The right-hand wall was full of
tall oblong windows, through which the view to the north could
be seen — the city, the blue waters of the Firth of Forth with,
beyond them, the shores of Fife and the snow-capped Lomond
Hills. It was a beautiful brisk February day, the sun fell on the
roofs of the capital with a shine not of gold but of platinum, the
white and luminous sunshine of the north.

Gilchrist, decently clothed in his blackest suit, his face as grey as those of the portraits above him, took his place at the foot of the table. Nobody had offered him a seat. He clutched the smooth round back of a mahogany chair in an effort to stop his hands from shaking.

'Have you anything to say before we start, Mr Gilchrist?' said the Chairman, lowering his spectacles and peering for the first time directly at his victim. He was not an unkind man, and he noted with a pity that his function could not allow him to indulge the unkempt, almost dirty appearance of his employee, his sunken cheeks, his soiled cuffs. Gilchrist looked ten years older, almost as if the hand of the Lord ... The Chairman suppressed the thought.

Gilchrist shook his head mutely. He had known this moment would come. To tell the truth he had willed it, and now all he wished was to be finished with it as rapidly as possible.

The Moderator himself rose at this point, intoning above the shuffling of papers — 'O Lord be present at our deliberations this afternoon and guide us in the paths of wisdom and mercy that no discord may inflame our hearts and that we may come to a decision compatible with both justice and compassion for thy truth's sake Amen.'

And how could they come to a decision that was compatible with both those things, thought Gilchrist savagely. Indeed, this was the whole problem, and what in earth or heaven could ever excuse the divine justice, the divine mercy, meted out to Alison Gilchrist?

He looked around him for some sign of sympathy on the faces of the four subinquisitors, all of whom had been for six years his own close associates. Their eyes were averted, with the exception of the only female present, a young woman of Welsh origin called Angharad Jones. She was attractive of shape and of dark eyes and hair, though in tongue and profile she was as sharp as a pick-axe. Help from that quarter would hardly assist him. Besides, she was gey young at 30 to be taken seriously by the rest of his reverend judges.

'We know — we were all saddened to hear — of your wife's untimely departure from this life. I believe she was also expecting a child, which must have been an additional blow. All I can say is

39

that we have prayed — I am sure I speak for all the members of the Board here present when I say we have prayed . . .'

Prayer! thought Gilchrist. Cannot these people see that the nature of God Himself is put in question by the evil he permits to stalk the world? And if that is so, to Whom, to what dark spirit, do we pray?

The Chairman's words emerged from above the hubbub of Gilchrist's thoughts: ' . . . however, despite our patience, you have hardly put in an appearance in this office during the last three months, and I am bound regretfully to admit that when you did so on those few rare occasions your breath, Mr Gilchrist . . .'

His tone was deeply reproachful. He had indeed been shocked and disappointed, saddened too, by his employee's behaviour. For the first few years of his employment, the young man had seemed so responsible, so willing, to have such promise. There was no doubt some basic instability in him, perhaps a trace of non-Scottish blood.

' . . . and I am bound to say also your speech, your, eh, equilibrium . . .'

The Moderator could be heard from the end of the table, loudly clicking his tongue.

Gilchrist could not deny it, even to others. That day in November when he had entered the chairman's room to discuss Professor McTaggart's projected new history of John Knox, *Knox Reborn* as it was officially to be called — *Knox Rebored*, or *Knox and It shall Be Opened Unto You*, as it was colloquially known in the office . . . Gilchrist had tacked into the chairman's bureau like a caravelle, heeling under its cargo of Belhaven and Famous Grouse. He had clutched at the nearest filing cabinet — surreptitiously, he had hoped. The cabinet was unlocked, however, and as it capsized its drawers shot open, catapulting much of their contents over the chairman's carpet. The manuscript he was carrying sprayed its sheets over and among these files and finally, to top the wreckage, came Gilchrist himself, sprawling, swamped, dismasted.

White Blood! His cargo had shifted. (It could have happened to anyone.)

To make matters worse, when three secretaries and four

cleaning ladies had finally picked up the flotsam and jetsam and sorted it, it was discovered that the manuscript Gilchrist had jettisoned was not that of the Reverend McTaggart at all, but one of the company's more profane projects, namely a book of advice to the laity on the working of the Partner Exchange System, and that the epoch-making McTaggart manuscript was nowhere to be found.

Gilchrist had to admit that the Board had been remarkably patient.

The Moderator himself now took a hand, cutting Gilchrist short in mid-sentence. He rose to his feet, thus elevating the level of his head to at least six and a half feet above carpet level, and cleared his throat just in case anyone might not have noticed the fact.

'I understand, Mr Gilchrist, that you were granted a month's leave of absence by your employers immediately after that sad event. Perhaps you would confirm that this is so? Very well then, the question which crosses *my* mind, Mr Gilchrist, is: How long do you want? Two months, three, six, a year? Employers have their rights too, you know.'

In his youth the Reverend Sinclair Duguid had been an amateur boxer, one of those burly Christians who could hold the Lord's corner as staunchly as any backslider could Satan's. He had been suspected on occasion of deliberately picking a quarrel with some foul-mouthed collier and forcing him to apologise (through a bruised jaw and a couple of broken teeth) to the Redeemer for taking his name in vain. To these two confident cards — his sense of physical and spiritual infallibility — he had now added the agreeable assurance of power. He had a broken nose, a bull-like lift to his head, and it was rumoured that his thick curly hair (still jet-black at the age of 50) concealed a pair of horns, like Moses. His great height was doubly intimidating for someone of Gilchrist's generation. The children of the twenty-first century, stunted by the glandular effects of fall-out, rarely reached a stature greater than 5 feet 2 inches. Men of the Moderator's generation, born in the last good years o the previous century, would murmur that their children were not Scots but Squats.

There seemed little Gilchrist could reply, though the

churchman's tone enraged him. He was being treated like a child of 9, not a man close on 30.

'However,' Duguid continued, 'there are even more serious charges to be laid at your door. If you will permit me, John,' and the Moderator glanced with purely formal deference at the Chairman who in turn muttered, 'Not at all, not at all,' without even a pretence that he had any choice in the matter.

'The problem, Mr Gilchrist, is of long standing. Well before the unfortunate death of your wife you were in charge of our series on late twentieth-century thought, one of which you had actually set about writing yourself, though in what sort of alcoholic haze I can barely bring myself to imagine. Perhaps indeed that explains it, for I have always thought that Satan finds intoxication particularly handy to his purposes. Perhaps our cousins the Muslims after all . . . Well, come now, Mr Gilchrist, don't stand there silent as a dummy, tell me what you have to say in answer to these charges.'

'What charges?' stammered Gilchrist.

'Surely you cannot fail to understand my meaning? Can your conscience be so far corrupted that . . . Why, I can hardly force the word from my lips, Mr Gilchrist, but since you insist. Science, Mr Gilchrist, science. The message of the Devil has somehow got into these books of yours, this one by Za—Za—Zaleski. And this tattered manuscript that I suppose you will admit to recognising?'

Duguid cast a pile of well-thumbed papers on the table. It did look uncannily like Gilchrist's own typewriting that covered them. It must indeed be the first draft of his aborted project *God and Twentieth-Century Science*.

'A very, eh, serious piece of work, Moderator,' put in Angharad in Gilchrist's defence. 'Studiously low key. Nothing frivolous about it.'

'That is precisely what perturbs me. Now if you had been ridiculing these ancient superstitions, then there might have been something to say for the undertaking, though it is my opinion that even poking fun at the Devil is dangerous, since it draws people's attention to his presence among us.'

'Forgive me, Moderator,' said Angharad, 'but that is not quite accurate. If you had read the book more carefully you would have seen that twentieth-century science had plenty to say about God.'

Duguid said softly, so as to make it appear that her voice had been raised too tartly, 'Are you claiming, Miss Jones, that I have not *read* this manuscript?'

The laws of debate forbid one to make such an insinuation, and Duguid turned back towards Gilchrist in triumph. 'In any case it is not myself alone but also the Science Research Interface, whose job is to approve acceptable technological work — I have shown this farrago to them, and they unanimously condemn it. It is unpublishable.'

'I don't see what's so wrong with it,' said Gilchrist, speaking up at last. 'It merely deals with twentieth-century theories of cause and effect — cause and fall-out, as we say now.'

'It deals, sir,' said Duguid, 'with *quantum physics.*' The words tasted horrible, and an expression of disgust crossed his face as he bit them out. 'Do I have to remind you at your age of the history of the last fifty years? Do I have to remind you that when government in Scotland collapsed after the Holocaust, the religious communities had to take over the tending of the sick, the distribution of food, the control of the police and the courts? That we have held these powers ever since as a duly constituted federal theocracy? That, aware of the lethal damage done to mankind by hatred and dogmatism, it is an article of our constitution that unfailing tolerance must be exercised in matters of the spirit? But that tolerance cannot be extended to the works of Satan, which brought about that terrible disaster in the first place?

'Physics, sir, above the nineteenth-century level, is not taught in our schools. The works of twentieth-century physics have been hunted down and destroyed, save for unique and single copies which are kept under lock and key in the *Enfer* of the National Library of Scotland, and some of us hope that one of these days the *Enfer* may prove true to its name by bursting into spontaneous combustion, so taking with it the Devil's work it holds. For if once the knowledge contained in those books were to get out, if man were to become capable once more of the madness of nuclear physics – ' (A spasm of pain passed across his face again) – 'then who could say what further horrors might burst upon the Earth?'

The inquisitors all yawned in syncopated time, for this was all too familiar to them. Once launched, however, nothing could quell a Duguid sermon.

'Do you not recall, sir, how Oppenheimer, himself one of the demoniacs who invented the Bomb, declared on witnessing its first explosion – and I take his words to be an admission of his own Satanic inspiration – "I am become Death, the exterminator of Worlds"? And how it is recorded in Holy Writ that the Lord cast Adam out of Eden for eating the fruit of the Tree of Knowledge?'

'Moderator,' said Gilchrist respectfully, 'may I say a word or two to defend myself?'

'Of course!' replied Duguid, a hint of surprise in his tone, for whatever could have made Gilchrist suppose he wasn't being listened to? 'Naturally! That is why we have convened you. Proceed, we are all attention.' He sat down heavily and, hooking his right hand round his ear, began to listen with an expression of bull-like obstinacy upon his face.

Gilchrist began to explain. His voice, hesitant at first, soon took on a more courageous tone as he warmed to his topic. Unfortunately, the subject was very obscure. His listeners in this year of grace 2036, knew less of physics than a 10-year-old schoolboy had fifty years earlier. The only thing the two had in common was their equal resistance to hearing about it. The concepts were strange – they could only have been born of the imagination of a raving lunatic. To mention just two or three of the things that Gilchrist said made you want to reach for the telephone and contact a vicar of the Church of Sigmund Freud.

The table they sat at, Gilchrist told them, was not solid, but more than 99 per cent empty space. It consisted in fact of tiny particles, like planets flying around their suns, but unimaginably minute.

(The Chairman tested the table with his hand, somewhat puzzled.)

Each particle, said Gilchrist, could be in several places at once

44

or travelling at several speeds at the same time. Reality was basically indefinite.

(The inquisitors looked at each other and shook their heads.)

... until you looked at the particles, when they turned out to have either a speed or a position in space. So *you* decided which they had. It was consciousness that collapsed uncertainty into reality.

(Sinclair Duguid remembered Bishop Berkeley, but he set the thought on one side.)

Such particles might also move backwards in time — briefly — thus infringing the laws of causality.

But they were not, Gilchrist said (thereby contradicting himself) so much particles as waves. What were they waves in? They were waves in probability. The world was nothing but a vast game of chance.

(What sort of thing, wondered Angharad, was probability? Could you kiss it?)

(Sinclair Duguid was heard to murmur, unaware that Einstein had said the same a full century before, 'God does not play dice.')

But to return to consciousness, said Gilchrist. Since the world is not made real till someone contemplates it, it consists till that moment of a gamut of different possibilities. The world is not a single world, but a 'superposition', an overlapping multitude of different worlds, all existing in parallel ... till someone looks at them, when a single unitary world is actualised — poof! — like a genie out of a bottle. As if your friend John didn't exist until you looked at him, when he suddenly materialised — bang! — out of what had been, till then, a flock of question marks, a cloud of ghosts, a multitude of 'Might-be-Johns'.

(Angharad laughed.)

So incredible is the whole thing, he said, that some authorities have suggested that, instead of all the possible worlds evaporating every time an actual world emerged from them, *all* the possible worlds were there *all* the time. The world is like an ever opening fan, it branches, it branches. Every time a single electron can be in two places, it *is* in two places, but in two separate worlds, so that the world is continually reproducing itself, creating more and more worlds, all existing at once, all existing in parallel. In this world, here, I pick up this pen and throw it on the table. In the next world, there, which has just split off from this one, I have not picked up the pen, I have not cast it across the table.

So perhaps when we make a decision, we don't make it, that is to say all the different alternatives we might choose are represented in different worlds. Perhaps there are other worlds just like this one, in which Herr Fleisch didn't invite the Russians in, in which there wasn't a war, in which the Communist *coup d'état* of 1917 never happened, in which the atom bomb was never invented. Perhaps . . .

Duguid had softened his manner a little. 'Very well, Mr Gilchrist,' he said, 'everything you say is very interesting. But what has it to do with Our Redeemer? It is hardly very *relevant*, for only the Lord's mercy is relevant. What has it to do with truth? It hardly seems very likely, does it? Rather some sort of fantasy world — "science fiction", I believe it used to be called — invented by a set of very clever, but deluded, men. My own advice to you, Mr Gilchrist, would be to get some help. You have obviously gone through a trying time these last few months, and some professional advice from one of our ministers, someone experienced in mental breakdown . . .'

Gilchrist had been aware that it was absurd to present any case for his book. He felt as ridiculous as if he had been Einstein trying to explain relativity to a coven of witch doctors — or rather, the boot was on the other foot, and he was more like a witch doctor expounding the poison oracle to Einstein.

'Well,' he said weakly, 'I cannot agree that our ancestors were mad. Mad in one way, since they brought the Holocaust upon us. But the very fact they did so proves their theory worked. A disaster, but work it did.'

'You are claiming truth for this rigmarole, then?' said the Moderator in a strange tone. Gilchrist realised that it was pitying. Why not? What he had done this afternoon had merely been the culminating act in five months of self-destruction.

'Mr Gilchrist, I say this with genuine regret,' said Duguid, saying it with genuine regret, 'but Paul reminds us: "Be not drunk with wine, wherein is excess; but be filled with the Spirit." Nor is that the whole of the story, for in the same Epistle it is written that we must "have no fellowship with the unfruitful works of darkness, but rather reprove them". No doubt we are all backsliders, for "there is none righteous, no, not one", but there is little we can do for someone who wishes to use this publishing house for the propagation of Satanic paradox.'

Thus Gilchrist, in the most Christian manner possible, received the sack.

5
Where Am I?

And as he journeyed, he came near
Damascus; and suddenly there
shined round about him a light
from heaven.

ACTS 9:3

Jenny Blinkbonny paced to and fro at the foot of the steps, tracing out a cat's cradle of short and jagged lines upon the pavement. Each time she stopped and set off in a new direction, her movements were so definite they seemed like a final decision to depart. After twenty paces or so, she would pause, turn in her tracks, her gaze would flicker from seventh floor window to entrance hall, she would glance at her watch, and set off again in a new direction. Did it take so long to give someone the sack? She did hope Peter hadn't lost his temper. Or — hope against hope — had they somehow been persuaded to reinstate him after all? She crissed and crossed the broad pavement, looking in her helmet and oversuit for all the world like a mechanical toy into which some inventor had fitted a perpetual motion device.

The lights from within the glass-panelled door, casting their rhomboid patterns on the pavement, were several times obscured from within. The door would swing wide, a radsuited figure would emerge. She would pause and wait expectantly, only to resume her pacing as she saw that it was not Gilchrist.

The hour struck, the quarter, and the half. It began to snow, reluctantly — a parsimonious, penny-pinching snow that shivered as it dropped in niggardly flakes through the biting wind. It was only when six o'clock came that, at last, a familiar patched and shabby radsuit sidled from the door. It stood there indecisively, its helmet turning from left to right. Jenny felt a stab of pity and affection. She halted in her pacing, and stood transfixed, gazing towards the steps.

The radsuit approached her, doubtfully.

'Jenny?'

'Yes, did you ...? What did you ...?'

'The sack,' said Gilchrist indistinctly from inside his helmet. 'They've given me the sack.' She could not get a glimpse of his face, but she had a horrible feeling there was satisfaction in his voice.

'Och, *Peter*,' she wailed. 'What did they say? Are you sure? Did you tell them ...?' For of course he wouldn't have, the silly bairn!

'I need a drink,' he said. 'You won't refuse me a drink, today of all days. You're not going to get on your high horse and stop me ...'

From celebrating disaster, she thought to herself.

'No, Peter,' she said, for this had all been thought out and prepared for. 'You can have your drink. Archie Rimmon ...' She didn't like Rimmon but this time he had done the right thing. Perhaps it was because he always did the right thing that she disliked him. Anyway, he had insisted that Peter, and she, and any friends they might care to bring along, would be welcome at Heriot Row. The consoling presence of those closest to him. Besides, it would keep him out of the hostelries for at least one night in the year. She had to admit it was a perfectly decent, thoughtful act. 'Judge not, that ye be not judged.'

But one can't help judging, and Jenny knew very well that a moderately prosperous and successful man like Rimmon would not be having two penniless secondary teachers and a freshly sacked editor to dinner, if it were not for an ulterior motive. That motive was, for the time being, her friend Helen Bannerman, who had moved in with the publicist two months earlier.

'But first we must pick up Alec. He'll be just round the corner in the Deacon's Den.'

Or perhaps not, she thought. He's been behaving oddly these last few weeks, almost as if he were jealous. But had she given him any cause for jealousy, any cause to think that she *belonged* in any way to him?

Alec indeed had been in two minds. But he had said to himself, If I'm not there, and if ... So they did find him in the pub, though gloomy, perhaps a little watchful.

Half a pint on into the evening, a radsuit entered backwards, doing a nervous two-step as it removed its helmet. The skull thus revealed was covered, though rather irregularly, with hair like tufts of bleached marsh-grass. Swivelling, it showed the profile of Virgil who, because he had arranged to meet them here, giggled with embarrassment on seeing them.

'How *melancolico*,' he assured Gilchrist, wringing his friend's hand guiltily. 'I wish I could have done something.'

'What could you have done?' asked Gilchrist in surprise, as they left the tavern to find a horse-drawn cab. But Virgil continued to feel exquisitely guilty for being the *kind of person* who could have done nothing.

The secret of Edinburgh New Town is that its exteriors are so grey, so nordic, so calm. Its spirit is the reverse of gothic. The vertical shapes of a medieval cathedral soar upwards, bursting into the frozen waterfall of a buttress, the daring exhilaration of a pinnacle, emphasising air and space more than the stone of which they are built. But the gothic cathedrals are the dwelling of an unknown god, born of a belief in the impossible. In them, gravity overcomes itself, has found a language to suggest its own opposite − speaking in stone of heaven, as mystics speak in words of the ineffable.

The eighteenth-century house has none of these flights of fancy. Its balance is that of poise, and not of flight. Its verticality is merely a set of flat planes, matter-of-fact and commonsensical. Yes, the floors rear above the street to the number of four or five, underlining their achievement by digging out a basement and setting it about with a schiltron of sharp-tongued railings. But they rise flatly, as if to admit that if they stepped out of line they would be punished. Uprightness is the law of nature as reason is the law of God, and an Edinburgh townhouse perfectly combines morality with the principles of Newton. Religious pragmatism observes Occam's razor, which shaves off all unnecessary excrescences, eschews all decoration.

And yet, tucked away at centre right, there is an elegant little Ionic portico, full of feeling or at least sensibility. Its mouth emits a couthie brightness, casting a welcoming carpet of orange light onto the snowy steps before it. Is this hypocrisy? Is it the spirit of Deacon Brodie, all things to all conditions of men? No, there is an inside and an outside to everyone. We all lead a double life.

Rimmon appeared, his lips carefully curved. Because of their configuration his smile was much narrower than other people's. Behind him, Helen hovered, nervously aware that she was not yet really the mistress of this house. From the room at the left of the hall the sound of two young male voices came:

' . . . gates of the Fortress of Doom . . .'

' . . . challenged by a werewolf . . .'

'Do you want to turn left or right?'

'Archie's sons spend all their time playing Dungeons and Dragons,' explained Helen, coming forward at last.

'They do attend church, though,' said Rimmon.

'Hardly any better, is it?' said Helen. 'Von Däniken's mystery tours, 9 a.m. every Sunday. Did you know,' she asked the guests, 'that according to the Kirk of Freud and Von Däniken, Heaven is situated on a planet in the Pleiades? And when you die you are transported there by spacemen? Did you know people call it the Kirk of Unidentified Phallic Objects? It's a truly fascinating religion!'

Well, thought Jenny, she must feel confident of herself after all if she's poking fun at her master and provider's church.

But Rimmon treated all kirks, including the one for which he worked, with the same ironic distance. 'Aye,' he said, 'it turns out that a Freudian dream is simply about landing on the Moon. But come along up to the sitting room, and have something to keep the rocket motors burning.'

'Can I give you a hand in the kitchen?' said Jenny, for she was longing to take her friend aside and learn all about . . . Rimmon had a couple of servants but, as she rightly guessed, this evening it was one of Helen's command performances.

The three men followed Rimmon up the staircase to the sitting room which was, in the old Scottish tradition, situated on the first floor — a vast and lofty ceilinged room, its shutters and curtains drawn against the snowy darkness, a fire blazing in its grate, its pictures, ornaments and furniture all speaking of a healthy bank balance. Rimmon sat listening to the report of the afternoon's

51

sacking with his usual polite detachment, though when Gilchrist began to describe his discussion with the Moderator, an uncharacteristic degree of interest began to show in his face. He began questioning Gilchrist on the accursed Einstein, on Bohr and Everett and Wheeler, until the other two men felt quite uneasy about this interest in diabolism. They were still talking about 'Schrödinger's cat' and 'Wigner's friend' when dinner was served. A sorcerer's familiars, Alec supposed.

The meal was served with beer. For wine was now unknown except as a word in the Bible, and folk talked these days of 'communion ale'. For dessert, however, Rimmon had an amazing delicacy to offer them: fresh oranges, purchased that morning at Leith docks off a boat that had sailed in from Morocco — purchased at a price that he took good care to tell them — 'Five pounds apiece, what do you think of that?'

'Active!' cried Jenny. She had never in her life tasted anything so exotic.

There's money to be made from kirks these days, thought Rimmon. Aloud, he said: 'The Lord will provide.'

Gilchrist had had, on leaving Redemption House, no intention of complaining about his treatment, for he recognised it was fair and that the Board, while a mite self-righteous perhaps, had at least no personal animus against him. As the beer went down, though, resentment began to surface.

'Duguid ... what a name! Quoting the Gospel at me, the old hypocrite. "Mr Gilchrist, my good sir," says he to me, "it is written by Saint Paul: 'Be not drunk with wine, wherein is excess; but be filled with spirits.' " Sorry, with the Holy Spirits,' he said, roaring with laughter.

The only one to defend him had been Angharad Jones, her dark Methodist eyes flashing with Welsh *hwyl*. The problem with women, he said, was that if they were pretty they were not taken seriously, and if they were not pretty they were a threat. Why had she bothered? He was a lost cause anyway.

Jenny felt jealous at this, though she knew that if she had been there she would not have opened her mouth.

Gilchrist then launched on a monologue about the wickedness of God — 'supposing he exists at all. As for his followers, does a belief in Him ever make the slightest difference to anyone's behaviour?'

Rimmon did not turn a hair. 'You really ought to try out Von Däniken's some time. We have such a spectacular ritual. Have I told you of the latest adjustments I've made to it? Coloured mock-ups of the Palenque rocketman. Oxygen masks. Pews shaped like rocket-ships, personalised dashboards for each worshipper, simulated blast-off and touch-down. A real feast for the imagination, I promise you.'

It was half past one before they left. The snow had stopped, and the streets were a glossy black and white, for it was thawing already. They waited on the pavement, listening for the clatter of hooves and grinding of wheels that would warn them of the approach of their carriage from the mews. For Rimmon had called his personal brougham for them — a typically correct and generous gesture, but done (Jenny wondered) for what motive? She had always known Kant to be wrong: a man who did something because he knew it to be right was not after all as good as one who did it because he wanted to be kind.

Up and down the road, nothing was stirring. The trees in Queen Street Gardens opposite stood as black and stark as skeletons against the glow of the city skyline. Some distance off, a solitary figure appeared round the corner from Howe Street and set off at an angle across the cobbles of Heriot Row. A walking snowman, one would have said, clicking his white stick upon the setts as he crossed the street. Curiously, the figure appeared not to be wearing a helmet, as if without it, he, a blind man, might be able to see.

The rumble could be heard of the approaching brougham.

The blind man had halted in the middle of the street, staring about him, uncertain which way to go to avoid being swept under the carriage wheels. His stick hovered in the air, held out almost horizontally as if it were a magic wand that would protect him. The coachman had seen him, and, soothing his mare, slowed her to a walk. Even so they passed within a hair's breadth of the blind man who, as he heard or sensed the horse stepping past him, swung round in alarm. The lights shone off his blind face, helmetless, white as the moon, and the mare, unfamiliar with men who did not wear helmets, still less familiar with men who did not have eyes in their heads, reared aside from him with a frightened whinny, and suddenly broke into a gallop. The coachman shouted, swayed in his seat, half rose, hauling on the reins. The brougham, swaying dangerously, careered at full tilt down Heriot Row towards the waiting group.

They for their part, seeing the danger, ducked back across the pavement and made for the safety of Rimmon's front porch. Except for Gilchrist, whose boot slipped on the wet snow as he turned. He sprawled half in the road, half out of it. The carriage was but twenty yards away now, and heading straight for the pavement edge.

Jenny tried to run back to help Gilchrist, but she was firmly held in the portico by Alec. She screamed, once, piercingly. Gilchrist, whose helmet had tumbled off into the gutter, saw the mare's iron hooves poised in the air above his head, with behind them the offside wheel of the vehicle heading straight for his face, its steel tyre spinning like a saw-blade. You know how such moments are. Time hovers motionless on an updraught of fear, and you are sharply aware of each minute detail — a fleck of slaver on the horse's flank, the black pits of its open nostrils, the cobbles shining like black and white satin, the glitter of snow-light on the brougham's brass rail. Through the coachman's visor the man's eyes could plainly be seen, staring in alarm at the impending accident. Gilchrist knew he was done for, about to be sheared apart on the hard stone roadway, and he had time to remember Alison and to be glad.

A jolt as if the very axle of the world had shifted, then a deafening crash of splintering wood and snapping springs. The hideous sound of a horse screaming with pain. The next thing Gilchrist knew — well, it was very odd. He was lying, not on the roadway at all, but halfway on to the pavement. Across the snow of the sidewalk, not one inch from his outstretched boot, the tracks of the carriage wheels could be seen steering straight for the basement railings. The brougham had smashed like a matchbox, the poor mare had impaled herself on the spears of the basement grille, the coachman had vanished altogether. Up and down the silent street, lights came on. Rimmon's door burst open, and he and Helen came out onto the steps.

Jenny broke away from Alec's grip, tears in her eyes, shouting, 'I hate you!'

Gilchrist sat up gingerly, feeling at his arms and legs, unable to believe that he was still whole and unharmed. Bewildered, he passed one hand across his face, inspecting it for signs of blood. Nothing. Suddenly Jenny was there, her helmet torn off too, crouching in the wet snow beside him, gazing into his eyes, asking again and again if he was all right.

'Yes, yes,' he kept saying in amazement. 'Yes, I think so.'

Rimmon, who had disappeared for a moment, returned with a shotgun to put the mare out of her misery. Meanwhile the others had discovered the coachman lying in a silent heap at the bottom of the basement well. When the carriage wheels had struck the kerb he had been projected over the horse's head like a sling-stone. Whether he was alive or dead was hard to say, but they knew better than to move him, and Helen telephoned for an ambulance. As for the blind man, by the time they started to wonder about him, he was nowhere to be seen, having vanished as if he had never existed.

When they had all discussed the accident with each other and with the neighbours — for such happenings are stimulating as well as shocking — they took it into their heads to wonder where Gilchrist was, and discovered him still standing on the edge of the kerb, deep in thought. He had made no move to put his helmet on, and was staring as if hypnotised at the point where the brougham had left the road.

'Peter,' said Jenny cautiously. When he made no reply, she approached him with the circumspection one uses to a sleepwalker, and touched his forearm with the tips of her fingers. 'Peter.'

Still no reply. But on his face there was an expression of the utmost bliss, as if he were witnessing a vision of angels, or such as came across the face of Thomas Traherne when he viewed the 'orient and immortal wheat'. His lips were moving softly, inaudibly, but when she bent her ear towards them, she could hear — or thought she could hear — him saying over and over again:

'That's it, that's it. How wonderful. Explains it all. Alison, Alison. God's mercy.'

A natural reaction in one who had had such a narrow escape, and was suffering from shock. Gilchrist was gently propelled back inside the house, still with the frown-lines smoothed from his forehead, still murmuring ecstatically to himself, and was offered a cup of herbal tea to restore him once more to the real world of cause and effect.

6

That Old Black Magic

*Preach the word; be instant
in season, out of season.*

—————— TIMOTHY 4:2 ——————

Saturday 9 February 2036

'Summertime', June 1939. The most hauntingly beautiful of all
Bechet's tracks, through which the meaning of suffering is told
without words, and understood. The soprano sax laments and
growls its requiem for — perhaps for Bechet's own grandfather, a
slave murdered for a crime he did not commit. Gilchrist, who had
been reduced to tears by every attempt to listen to this music
since Alison's death, was able after his experience of last night, to
attend to it again.

Soothed, released, as the music soared sublimely to its climax,
he switched off the magnetograph and turned to the shelves of
his bookcase. Where was it hidden? The little book that held the
secret, or rather the final link in the chain of truth, the final piece
in the puzzle of God's universe. The understanding that had
struck him last night in the snow, when the impossible had
happened and he, lying directly in the path of the approaching
carriage, had suddenly found himself removed from that fatal
place by inches of snow-covered pavement — that conviction
was still with him this morning. Effect had not followed cause,
and he knew why.

Ah, here it was. Alec had lent it to him some four months ago —
this piece of battered science fiction, the 1995 edition of Fred
Hoyle's *October the First is Too Late*. In the way of all borrowers
of books, he had never got round to returning it. You had to be
careful handling this copy, for it was a cheap edition over forty
years old and it was as if time were hot, and in its passing had

57

slightly singed the pages, making them dry and brittle. Gilchrist turned to page 74, and scanned the paragraphs rapidly.

That's it. Yes, he thought triumphantly, that's the answer.

It is perfectly clear how, normally, we see time. Our consciousness is bound to that single identity, that single amalgam of brain, mind, body and emotions that we call our selves. Our consciousness is bound also to successive moments of time which follow each other steadily, ineluctably, without possibility of their being run backwards or in any different order. We see our lives, therefore, something like this: the present moment is a little illuminated box of experience which, as we live it, is illuminated *now*. The last moment was the box of experience through which we have just been living, only the light of conscious awareness isn't on in that box *just now*; and the moment to come is just such another wee box, only the light hasn't come on in it *just yet*. That's how it seems, isn't it? So we have a picture of our own lives as a series — an enormously long series, millions upon millions of instants in length — of little boxes in sequence, one after another in single line ahead. Our sense of living a continuous existence is because each box contains memories of the earlier boxes. Our consciousness is like a light, shining into each box and illuminating its contents in turn, before moving on to the next one.

Yes, he said to himself, that's clear enough.

But at that moment there came a ring at the doorbell. Jenny?

Pulling the door open, however, Gilchrist was confronted by a quite unfamiliar face. Caught between the depth of his meditation and his expectation of seeing Jenny Blinkbonny's lively blue eyes, he was for a moment quite disoriented. Who . . .?

Then he saw the black book clasped tightly under one armpit, the bundle of leaflets clutched in the other hand, thrust officiously out towards him. A dark and bulky radsuit of indeterminate sex, topped by a grey-lined face, from which there stared two insistent brown eyes.

'I come from God,' said the woman in exactly the same tone as you would say 'I'm just away to the launderette.'

'I see,' said Gilchrist, and tried to shut the door. Too late. She had her foot in it.

58

He looked back into her eyes. Though they were staring straight at him, they were oblivious of his presence. That is to say, they could see a man in front of them, or rather not a man, but just a walking receptacle, an empty vessel, a potential convert.

'Brother, are you saved? Has the light of God shone into the darkness of your heart? Have you been washed clean in the Blood of the Lamb?'

'Eh — which particular kirk ...?' ventured Gilchrist. She was trying to push past him now, and since she was at least 40, she was taller than he. He found he had to lean bodily against her, such was the force of her assault. It was the diametric opposite of a tug-o'-war, but despite the absurdity of their position — she leaning forward at thirty degrees, he at nearly forty-five, each pushing each other and getting nowhere, her practised patter continued to resound over his head without even a catch in its breath.

'*Coitus reservatus*,' gabbled the evangelist. 'The divine hallucinogen. The message of Timothy Leary, of Gopi Krishna, of Henri Michaux, of Meister Eckhart ...'

'Have you got it quite right?' gasped Gilchrist desperately. 'Are you sure the message is the same?'

All was becoming clear, particularly as he had glimpsed the hatbox full of pills that she clutched in her left hand. A Huxleyite, one of those who believed in instant revelation. Swallow, and ye shall find.

'All, all agree that the world is Maya, that the Kama Sutra must be taken literally, that you must drink deep of the draught of mystic vision, for it is written "Purge me with hyssop and I shall be clean; wash me and I shall be whiter than snow." Divine *soma*!' she carolled, seizing him by the collar, twisting it and nearly upending him.

'They were pacifists, all pacifists!' croaked Gilchrist. 'What sort of a — white blood! — pacifist are you?'

'I need a noise!' the evangelist seemed to cry. No, Gilchrist suddenly realised, it must be 'Oneida Noyes!'

'Madam,' he pleaded, 'Please show some Christian restraint.'

'It is written, "Thou shalt become the instrument of divine

59

grace" and that means you!' She was shrieking like a mynah bird.

'You're taking the name of Henri Michaux in vain,' he shouted back.

Thank God! That had put her off balance for a moment. What? A man who had heard of Henri Michaux? Gilchrist took advantage of this sudden fit of doubt to knock the hatbox out of her hand, so that it flew backwards onto the landing of the common stair, and scattered its diversely coloured contents down the steps. A sound of terrible grief was torn from the woman's throat, like that of a mother seeing her toddler set off across a busy road. She grovelled in a fluster of tracts, scrabbling for her beloved pills, and Gilchrist, his heart in his mouth, slammed and bolted the door.

He stood behind it listening. After a minute or so, the letter-box opened, and a voice came through it cooing gently, 'Brother, do not harden your heart against the word of God! Think upon your own salvation, brother!' And then, after an unwilling pause, 'Please!'

'Go away!' shouted Gilchrist, loosening his collar and trying to catch his breath.

Ignoring the pleading tones from the letter-box, he stalked away down the hall to the sitting room, and picked up Hoyle again. It was his own fault. In these days of the holy rag trade, churches touting their instant salvation from door to door, you should never open up without first looking through the spyhole. To settle his mind again, he switched on the magnetograph, and the notes of 'I Know that You Know' came spilling out into the room, cooling his injured feelings, blowing them calm again in the fresh whirling breeze of the soprano sax. Each take was different, but each had the same sense of inevitability, as if every choice the saxophonist made created its own certainty. A willed deflection of sound from the 'right note', but bringing with it a sense of greater rightness. Improvisation — joy and freedom — or rather the joy *of* freedom, which the Indians call *ananda*. Free will, the secret *after all* of God's unfailing love and mercy. Alison, where are you at this moment? But he knew now that she was safe somewhere, of that he was utterly sure, lively and alive as he remembered her.

He thought of the sequence of little boxes, those myriads of instants of illuminated time that made up his destiny. We think of them as extending forward in a continuous, steady, single line. But what guarantees it is a *single* line? Naturally it appears so to us, for our consciousness is, at any given moment, but a single light in a single box. But what if the line is not single but is continually dividing, forking, bifurcating, cleaving, branching, ramifying. Box no. 45 say, is followed not only by Box 46A, but by Boxes 46B and C, which are alternatives; the light of consciousness divides too, following each of these divergent outcomes — these *doubtcomes*. And Box 46A is followed, not just by Box 47A, but by Boxes 47B and C, and consciousness divides once more, following, in three different worlds, three different destinies.

But is not that exactly how things seem to us? We are continually faced with decisions that we have to take, branching paths that present themselves before us. We know that whichever path we take, that one will turn out to be completely real. We suppose that the other ones, which we decided against, are at that moment of decision reduced to clouds and air. But is that so? Since the paths we choose always turn out to be real, it follows that either our choice *makes* reality, or else the alternative universes are all of them real!

Those scientific texts that he had so laboriously amassed over the years — a coverless book in somebody's attic, a volume found on a rubbish heap, a whole cupboardful of treasures rescued in secret from a ruined house — what did they say? That the world is not a single definite reality, but a curious overlapping combination of all its alternative possibilities. Which alternative world will appear is entirely the choice of the observer. So it is the human act of choice which selects and realises each of these alternatives. But it is equally plausible to suppose that there is a multiplicity of co-existing worlds, and in one of them I choose one thing, in another something quite different.

That feeling of infinite possibility, that belief that we might act differently, that feeling that we have a universe of other selves hidden within us.

Yes, yes, it feels so right.

61

Moreover it explains that unbelievable, that impossible truth — for we know it, we see it around us — that Scotland, alone of the nations of the world, has survived — despite the Bomb, despite being drenched in fall-out and ravaged by filthy pestilence. We are here, and yet how can we be here unless, in our world, the well-nigh impossible has actually happened — the chance in a million million?

But now, what happens if, when I reach Box no. 79, the two boxes that confront me are Box no. 80A and Box no. 80B, and in 80A my conscious life continues, whereas in 80B I am dead? He turned to that point in the book where Hoyle proposed a kind of 'thought experiment'.

'Hook up a bomb which explodes according to whether you have the decay of a nucleus or not. Make the bomb so big that it becomes a doomsday machine. Let it be capable — if exploded — of wiping out all life on Earth. Let the whole thing go for a critical few seconds, you remember we were considering whether a nucleus would decay in a particular ten seconds. Do we all survive or don't we?

'My guess is that inevitably we appear to survive, because there is a division, the whole world divides into two, into two completely disparate stacks of pigeon holes. In one, a nucleus undergoes decay, explodes the bomb, and wipes us out. But the pigeon holes in that case never contain anything further about life on Earth. So although those pigeon holes might be activated, there could never be any awareness that an explosion had taken place. In the other block, the Earth would be safe, our lives would continue . . .Whenever the spotlight of consciousness hit those pigeon holes we should be aware of the Earth and we should decide the bomb had not exploded.'

Exactly. And that was the key to it all. Now that he had found the secret — the ultimate secret — Gilchrist wondered why he had never seen it before. It looked so definite now, so self-evident. Thoughtfully he repeated the words, 'My guess is that inevitably we appear to survive.' Was that not exactly what had happened to him, the night before — no, this very morning, at half past one? The world had divided into two — one world in which he, Gilchrist, had been killed, and another in which the carriage had hit some obstruction, had swerved aside, had 'miraculously' spared him.

For think of what must happen — yes, *must* happen — if you reach a point in your headlong descent of the river of lighted boxes, the necklace of lighted pearls, where the paths diverge, but the left-hand path is black, empty, devoid of consciousness, where it is death that awaits you. What if the right-hand track is lit, and on that track your life goes on? Clearly you would never know you would have died, because, for *you*, for *your* consciousness, as far as *your* life is concerned, the left-hand track does not exist. In short, where two paths offer themselves, and one is death, my consciousness *must* continue along the path of life!

Gilchrist walked to the window and looked out, but automatically. He did not see the tabby cat preening itself on the wall opposite, the children playing at space-invaders, the Huxleyite evangelist emerging from number 27. His attention had withdrawn from the messages of his eyes and concentrated instead on the image cast inside his mind, upon some disembodied screen — a diagram of lines, bifurcating, forking, parting, splitting into 2, then 4, then 8, then 16, 32, 64 ... It shifted and became a map of branching paths which moved and entwined like snakes as he watched them. It shifted again and became a tree, a tangle of shoots and branches seeking the light. It shifted again and became the criss-crossing droplets left by particles in a twentieth-century cloud-chamber.

The front door bell rang again, and Gilchrist jumped. Was the Huxleyite back? He remembered now that he had just seen her, seen her without noticing, crossing the street.

But, peering through the spyhole, a much more welcome sight met his eyes. He threw the door wide, smiling (and it felt as if this was the first time in six months that he had smiled), holding his arms open.

Jenny looked at him with pleasure, then with slight concern. 'Peter, you look positively happy!'

'And so I should, my dear,' he said, embracing her and drawing her inside. 'I have just solved the problem that for three thousand years ...'

She looked at him warily as he told her. Had he taken leave of his wits?

'... that for three thousand years has puzzled the world's greatest minds. I have just solved the problem of good and evil!'

7

Easy Rider

*Then was Jesus led up of the
spirit into the wilderness to
be tempted by the devil.*

———————— MATTHEW 4:1 ————————

Loch Broom, Friday 29 February 2036

Though the population of Scotland was now but 3 million, the Highlands were more densely populated than they had been a century before. Thousands had fled northwards to escape the anarchy that for a decade had made the cities places of violence, terror and starvation. Skye, Morar, Torridon, Coigach, Morvern, Assynt — at one time the heartland of the Wee Frees — were now a patchwork of small communities, each with its own eccentric rites and dogmas. To add to this variety, the 'Pilgrim Fathers' had landed in the autumn of '98 — refugees from the destruction of America's eastern coasts — and these immigrants in reverse had set up a number of colonies on the Hebridean seaboard where the strange twanging sounds of American speech could be heard to this day — as if the people there suffered from permanent transatlantic catarrh.

This was the region to which Gilchrist was headed now, having left the steam train at Inverness and taken the electrobus, rocking and humming its way westwards through Strath Conon, Strath Garve and Braemore, all the way to the head of Loch Broom. A gentle, fertile land at first, by the time you reached Lubfearn it was the wilderness — a landscape scattered with boulders, so many you might think they were the bleached white skulls of clansmen who had lain here since some ancient massacre — a wilderness of bog and moorland, of stags and buzzards, with the snow-capped mountains gaining continually in size as they moved ever westwards, and Gilchrist's eyes held transfixed in sheer pleasure at the sight. Before him now a loch stretched away like a long blue arm pointing at the peak of An Teallach cutting jaggedly into the sky ahead. To the right the barren snow of Ben Dearg rose upwards against a backcloth of black cloud. The mountain itself, however, was drenched in sunlight, so that it looked as if it had been cast in metal by a silversmith. For a moment time seemed to slip and shift, and Gilchrist might have been one of his own ancestors a hundred and fifty years ago, gazing out of a bus at this very point, viewing the wilderness out of which had come the invading Highland clans of the Forty-Five — out of which soon there would come a prophet to make new the way of the Lord.

The sunlight through which they rode was suddenly gone, banished by a single gust of wet Atlantic wind. All sight was blotted out as the black clouds pounced upon the bus and enveloped it in a flurry of pouring snow, so dense it was like a fog.

Intellectual rhymes with ineffectual, and Gilchrist was (so Rimmon had thought) an unstable waster. Rimmon never used the word 'friendship' except aloud and to others. Had it not been for Helen — and aye, she was worth wasting a few months over — so perfectly plump and blonde, her naked thighs the colour and texture of fresh cream . . . When she had brought him word of this 'revelation' she supposed Gilchrist to have had, he had thought it laughable.

A week later he was not so sure. Gilchrist had been seen in the Grassmarket, sober and lucid, preaching from a soapbox. Some folk had even listened. He went down himself on the following day and stood in the background, judiciously.

Interesting. Fascinating, even. But no way to launch a new religion. For it isn't truth or reason — or even conviction — that matters. The man needed to sit down quietly and work out — no, not his theory, but its method of presentation. Only persuasiveness persuades, and he, Archie Rimmon, knew all about that. Was he not publicity agent for the Cult of Freud and Von Däniken?

Worth pursuing. Some spare evening hour that would have been wasted anyway. Besides, it kept the lass contented for a wee while longer. Gilchrist and Jenny had been invited again to dinner. This time there were peaches ('How did he do it?' they exclaimed) as amazing as a fruit from Aldebaran.

Afterwards Rimmon congratulated himself. To his surprise the hours of discussion had passed like minutes. He had felt no excitement, for that was not his way, but yes, others might find it exciting. It remained to be seen what could be made of it. If only the man could put his thoughts in order!

But — and this impressed him — Gilchrist knew this already. Indeed, he put his head on his knees at one point and practically wept in public because he had a message, and that message was the truth, but his audience wouldn't listen.

'I know a cure for that,' Rimmon had said. 'A period of thought, that's the thing, a period of retreat from the world. It has to be hard work, mind. *When* you have put your thoughts in order, *then* come back and talk to me.'

'But you are a devotee of Von Däniken . . .'

'Are you interested in telling people the truth, or not?' asked Rimmon. 'For that, you must get them to see it.'

A period of stock-taking. He, Rimmon, knew just the place. And just the person.

Gilchrist's gaze, blocked by the grey-white curtain of snow, fell upon the girl in the seat opposite. She was a little too fat, a little puffy round the eyes, and pale as a leukaemia patient.

The moment he looked at her she leaned forward, and breathed, 'Say, man, what's your kirk? Guess you're a Caledonian Israelite.'

Such were the formalities of greeting between the sexes in twenty-first century Scotland.

'Tribe of Manasseh,' said Gilchrist, gazing at her solemnly.

'You're a Mackenzie, then? Or maybe a Menzies?' She pronounced this correctly as Ming-iss, but she had all the naïve excitement of the American Scot in identifying a clan.

'And what are you? Are you a Levi, like the Jeans?'

'Yeah, I'm called Jean,' she replied, completely mistaking his drift. But then, few people had Gilchrist's learning, his breadth of reading, his knowledge (for instance) of obscure twentieth-century garments.

67

As she rattled on, Gilchrist savoured her vowel sounds — and certain other peculiarities in her speech — with delight. Why, it was a piece of the past restored! She must be the daughter of some Pilgrim Father of '98, and as such she was a fragment of pickled and nasalised history. An accent almost incomprehensible, consigned to destruction, as rare as Gaelic or French!

'No *sir*, I'm an Ecclesiast.'

'An Iconoclast?'

'No, an Ecclesiast.'

Gilchrist brooded upon this information. ' "Vanity, saith the preacher, all is vanity"?' he brought out at last.

The lass giggled engagingly. 'No *sir*. The Ecclesia of Eros and Agape. Pure release from sin. I gotta tell you. Pure release from all your complexes, neuroses, paradoxes and psychic hang-ups.'

'Agape' came out as 'Eggapay', complexes as 'caamplixes', 'I gotta tell you' as 'Ahgatta till yuh', 'paradoxes' as 'perodaxes' like the name of some flying dinosaur. All the vowels shoogled round in an eightsome reel! And that ear-splitting nasal whine!

Another cult for his collection! 'What are your rites?' he asked softly, leaning forward in his turn, for perhaps there was some fanatic of the Covenant of Anorexia within earshot, and they approved of nothing, from eating, through speech between strangers, to ... 'If whatever-it-is offend thee, cut it off.'

'Oh, they're fess naten,' said the pale plump lass. 'The kiss of peace has nothing on us. Halleluyah! You should get off at Loch Broom and meet the congregation.' She pronounced the 'ch' properly too, but the vowels ... As a matter of fact, Gilchrist admitted to himself, these distorted sounds had a certain attractiveness about them. The girl radiated sex. He thought of Jenny.

'I am impressed,' said Rimmon, aware that to make himself *seem* impressed he had to turn his head so that his eyes shone briefly in the light. Even when his feelings were at their most sincere, he mourned to himself, folk misunderstood him.

'I am impressed,' he repeated. 'I believe you have made an important discovery.'

68

'An?' thought Jenny to herself. 'The!'

'Our people,' said Gilchrist slowly and thoughtfully, 'our demoralised human race. The message ... The truth will set us free.

'But I don't see how to do it. I don't see my way clear. How to *say* it. Besides, there are problems in the theory itself. When somebody dies, that is clear, for the ways part, they continue along another of the infinite paths of God. But when somebody suffers, aye, that's a harder thing.'

'I see the problem,' agreed Rimmon. He waited.

Gilchrist beat gently on the tapestried arm of Rimmon's chair. 'But I'm sure there's an answer.'

'Aha,' said Rimmon, 'and if you're sure, then you'll find it, won't you?'

'Och yes,' replied Gilchrist. He seemed very certain, thought Rimmon, and how encouraging that was!

'To tell the truth, my name begins with a G, so I'm the tribe of Gad,' said Gilchrist.

'The tribe of God?' said she in puzzlement, for by 'Gad' she meant 'God'.

'Never mind, tell me about your rites. I'm sure they're much more exciting than my name.'

'They're sure eck saaten,' said Jean in a husky whisper. As she listed the colourful details, her blush deepened, her eyes grew darker, her lips more moist.

' ... a cottage I own,' said Rimmon. 'Up in Assynt among the mountains, by the shores of Eddrachillis Bay. The perfect place for retreat, meditation, the occasional mystical experience. You'll be able to think things over in perfect tranquillity.'

'It does sound beautiful,' agreed Jenny, her eyes shining.

'I am confident that, there, God will speak to you again. But that is not the most important point. There is someone who will be of great interest to you. He will be able to clear up any small questions of detail — of "doctrinal" detail, one might say. I'll give you a letter of introduction.'

'Who . . .' wondered Gilchrist. Then, light dawning, 'You can't mean . . .!'

'Indeed I do. It's where Zaleski stays.'

'What? The Satanist who sent me that manuscript?'

'*He* calls himself a quantum physicist. A dying breed. Those who were not lynched in '98 are mostly in their graves by now. Or else they have changed their names, recanted, embraced some piping hot gospel or other. But not Zaleski. Now, if there are any problems in the doctrine . . .'

'Active!' said Gilchrist in delight.

Rimmon brushed aside their effusive thanks. People amused him. They always imputed altruistic motives to one's actions, whereas it was merely a small commercial risk he was taking. At the end of the day there might be no profit, but then his investment at this stage was minute.

He wondered, however, if it would be practical to dissuade Jenny from going too. He must see if he couldn't manipulate that teacher Jamieson back into her favour since, in his experience, debutant Messiahs had their most creative ideas when sexually most frustrated, and full-blown Gods were most charismatic when they were bachelors.

Outside the electrobus, the squall of snowflakes had passed by, the clouds had lifted, torn ragged by the wind, and as they reached the top of the steep descent of Corrieshalloch, rifts of moving sunlight pursued each other across the flanks of the mountain as if from a series of small and hasty suns.

The plump pale girl had finished her exposé, patting her hair devoutly and exclaiming, 'Praise the Lord!'

'Remarkable!' said Gilchrist.

'It depends,' said the lass judiciously. 'But with the right person it can be . . . eck steddic! The real electromagnetic shock-wave!'

'But − I hardly know how to put this − but are mutants . . .?'

'Och no,' said Jean, scandalised. 'After all, the Kirk has its moral duties.'

Yes, Gilchrist could see it all. A church, exclusive to normals, where instant partner-exchange was sacramental, was the core of religious ritual. Its social utility was immediately obvious. To maximise the chances of fertility among the non-mutant population! While at the same time giving a sexual guarantee of religious ecstasy. He admired these people. They had their eyes set firmly on the future of the race.

'Why go on to Assynt?' she was asking him. 'Even if you were to stop off at Ullapool just till the Sabbath . . .' He was an attractive man, tall and upstanding (5 feet 2, she guessed), and . . . 'I bet you're furtle,' she flattered him.

Indeed, it was an offer not without its attractions, but just at present Gilchrist was a man ruled by an idea. Ruled too by his memories of Alison and his hopes of Jenny. Considering that, considering them, he told himself, this was a choice that only *one* of his alternative selves would make. That being so, he was happy not to agree, while yet knowing that that hundredth part of his own possibilities would make a different one, and would undutifully slip off the bus at Ullapool.

How effective my theory is, he thought, congratulating himself. Why, it works, it makes the right decision easier!

8

Dear Old Southland

Then if any man shall say unto you, Lo, here is Christ, or there; believe it not.

———— MATTHEW 24:23 ————

Drumbeg, Saturday 5 April 2036

At Drumbeg, at this season of the year, nothing is green. The marsh-grass, the flanks of the lochanside, the grassy cliffs slanting down to the shore, are golden brown under the blue sky — a sunburnt Spanish colour. Trees huddle in the crannies of the cliffs, leafless as yet and black. The waters of Eddrachillis Bay, as Jenny and Gilchrist stood gazing northwards, were ultramarine, scattered with countless islands. Still further to the north, crouched the peaks of Arkle and Foinaven, dressed in pure white, beached and stranded there like drift-ice from the Pole. They were somewhat hazy in the crystalline air, and so even was nearby Quinag, a miniature mountain range that dominated the eastern skyline. On such a day, the hills of the north take on an unreal look, as if they are projections cast upon the luminous sky out of some further reality. To the south, a strange and barren terrain surrounded them: mile upon mile of tumbled hillocks, through which the naked rock stared and glittered. Scattered among this desert chaos were countless tiny lochans like the broken fragments of some enormous mirror. And indeed, these napkins of wind-troubled water were remnants of the primeval ice-sheet. On the tops of the headlands reaching out towards the bay were isolated rocks of all shapes and sizes, looking like a herd of cattle grazing there, but turned to shapeless stone. These rocks were far from the mountains that gave them birth, having

72

been carried here afloat on the glaciers and, when the tide of ice retreated, left stranded where they still lie on the hilltops, confidently watching for the glaciers' return. For their time-scale is longer, far longer than that of the human race.

Jenny, her hand in Gilchrist's, gazed in silence, breathing in the clear cool breeze, and watched the flecks of foam crumbling on the shoreline of little Cul Eilean below. It was like standing inside a huge luminous crystal — as if this land had been preserved in diamond since long before human time began.

At last she turned to him and said: 'Is it always like this here?'

Gilchrist laughed. 'They have a saying, "If you like our weather, just wait for another ten minutes." It could be pouring with rain in half an hour's time — or more likely snow — and go on for a fortnight. There's no telling. It's a douce, unstable, sentimental climate.'

'I'm lucky, then?'

'*I'm* lucky,' he said, taking her in his arms. There was silence, while the wind-drenched sunshine of Assynt was blotted out. The tensions in their kissing were exciting — as yet excitingly unresolved.

'You haven't seen the cottage yet.'

'Has it got a name?' An idea struck her. 'Perhaps it's called the House of Rimmon,' she said, taken with a fit of the giggles.

'And Alec?' he said, as they went down.

'I told him I was going away for the Easter holiday. I didn't say where. No, I had more trouble with Archie.'

'Archie? Oh, Rimmon.'

For decency's sake they put their helmets on again as they entered the village. A black radsuit passed them, audibly counting. 'Five, four, three, two, one, zero.' At the count of zero he changed step and began again: 'A hundred, ninety-nine . . .'

Jenny at once knew what to think. 'What sect is that?' she asked with interest.

'They call themselves the Sum of God. "In the beginning was the logarithm . . ." It seems they scrub their hands in pure burn water six times a day, and . . .'

'But why is he counting?'

'It's to prevent himself having evil thoughts. I've noticed they

73

steer very clear of silent folk like you and me. They call us the Open-Minded — with horror, for any little aperture may let the Devil in. They're peculiar to the Highlands.'

'Then how can they take in all this?' she asked, waving her hand at the diamantine view.

'That's the whole point.'

Turning into a perilously steep little wynd between two cottages, they traversed it for fifty yards and came to two modern houses backed into the shadow of the cliff with a view over the islet-scattered bay.

'It's like a flock of birds all turned to stone,' said Jenny, lips parted, gazing at the spaced-out islands.

And here was the first sight of green — a clump of viridian spears, with the trumpets of daffodils arching out of them, and further off, the yellow eyes of primroses peering from an acid-green crinkle of leaves.

Their actions once they entered the cottage were dance- or trance-like — steps in an inevitable progress towards the bedroom. By her half lie to Alec, by coming here at all, Jenny had committed herself — at least to an experiment. And, as any sensible young lassie knew, experiment there had to be, for in a society where less than one-sixth of couples ever produced children, no one in their senses would reach matrimony unless they were already pregnant. There was, it is true, a sect that (with saintly honesty) called itself the Holy Saints of Hypocrisy, but their practice was no different from that of other people.

When you are naked and look directly into someone's eyes, it seems that consciousness directly contacts consciousness. This afternoon, for Jenny, it was as if her soul and her lover's had risen to the surface of their skin so that, embracing body to body, they had become as sensitive as mirrors to each other.

For Gilchrist, this was power and joy, an opening to his new life, Jenny the elegant frigate who would carry him there, and put the first successful seal on his decision. Her approbation was a promise — that later *he* would redeem the world. He made love impeccably, as you would make a speech — in time to the applause within his mind.

'Spikenard and saffron, calamus and cinnamon, with all trees of

74

frankincense ... a fountain of gardens, a well of living waters ...'
The mountains of myrrh in Solomon's Song, and the bedroom
drenched in warm musk.

'And Alison? Was she more ...?'

'Of course not!'

Much later, Jenny, flushed and bonny, raising herself on one
elbow, admiring herself in the mirror of Gilchrist's approval,
broached a practical question.

'Och yes, didn't I say? We're invited by our neighbour.'

'My God!' cried Jenny, jumping out of bed.

Stanislaus 'Zen' Zaleski was as his name suggested – no
ordinary West Highland neighbour. He looked like the photo-
graphs of the accursed Einstein in the banned biographies. His
hair was as long as a twentieth-century scientist's, and impres-
sively thick and white. A sage. A dishevelled magus of equation,
cyclotron and cloud-chamber. The very picture of a Satanist.
Jenny (though no Catholic) crossed herself in Roman fashion
when she set eyes on him, then, blushing crimson, apologised.

'Nonsense,' he said. 'It's my fault, going about like this,
frightening charming young ladies. I know I look like the Devil
himself, don't be put off.'

He ushered them into a sitting room whose centre was three
armchairs and a pair of coffee tables all placed round the focus of
a peat fire. Dark swathes of shadow lay in the further corners of
the room, and the night glowed purple-blue through the window.
So concentrated was the light of the two standard lamps shining
down on this central circle that Gilchrist thought for a crazy
moment of police cells and interrogations. The pleasant backcloth of a symphony, playing on the magnetograph, belied this.
Gilchrist wondered what it was. Mozart? Not something that he
recognised.

Zaleski took Jenny just above the elbow, by the sensitive velvet
of her inner arm, and led her to the best easy chair. 'Sit yourself
down, my dear, and tell me what you want to drink.'

Having served them both (Gilchrist took only soda) he
vanished to the kitchen, leaving Jenny, round-eyed, open-
mouthed, appealing to her man:

'Why does he talk like that?'

When Zaleski spoke, his mouth seemed full of moisture and squashy fruit. 'Nonshensh,' he had said. 'Fwaightening. Deown't be put awff.' He didn't pronounce his r's.

'You're a teacher of history, Jenny. Have you not heard Churchill on the records? Or Anthony Wedgewood Benn? Our host is a dinosaur.'

'Zen' returned, beaming with pleasure at hearing himself discussed. When Jenny said, 'It's not a Polish accent, then?' he burst into laughter.

'No, my dear, my family fled to Britain when the Communist—Nazi front invaded us in 1939, and we all went to very *private* English public schools. I was brought up a very aristocratic "deinashaw".' That was — oh, it's frightening to remember how long ago — I was born in '72, you know.' He was silent, gazing back in disbelief over the years.

'What's your theory, then?' asked Jenny, her lips as usual charmingly parted.

'Well, all the English upper class used to talk like me. My idea is that, back in the eighteenth and nineteenth centuries, people died young. Except the rich, the aristocrats. But even for aristocrats, there were no such things as false teeth. Hence the language that snobbish little children heard from their aged, aged grandparents was ... toothless.'

Well, he certainly knew how to laugh at himself, thought Jenny, quite taken by the old man.

Over dinner Zaleski explained about himself. In the '90s he had been a theoretical physicist at Glasgow University, where his wife also had worked in the biochemistry department. She, however, had been killed in the wholesale burnings of laboratories and lynchings of scientists that followed the dropping of the Bomb. He had escaped by the skin of his teeth and, having fled north, had supported himself as dominie in the local school till his retirement earlier this year. He had even married again, and his only daughter lived in Edinburgh. But he had been widowed for a second time ten years before. 'The usual thing, you know.'

Jenny in sympathy pressed her plump young hand upon his wrinkled old one.

' "Zen" has been so useful, darling,' said Gilchrist

enthusiastically. 'To have the theory straight from the horse's mouth . . .!'

'And is it all . . . *correct*?' asked Jenny, hardly daring to hope that it was.

'Oh yes, my dear, I can confirm that your Peter has got his facts quite right. Of course, he doesn't understand the mathematics, who does these days? But that doesn't matter. His presentation of these alternative universes is absolutely orthodox. Though Einstein, of course . . . Mind you, a lot of my colleagues – oh, the majority – didn't like such speculations. The maths was enough for them, they used to say. What does it matter what it means, providing it works? Science is just a tool, they used to say, don't ask it to tell you what the universe is really like. But I can't say I ever agreed with that.'

'Then you don't think he's dabbling in . . . in Satanism?'

Zaleski laughed. 'I'm a physicist, my dear. Or rather, I *was*.' An expression of sadness came over his face.

'But you must have some beliefs?'

'I don't believe in Satan, my dear, and that's for sure. But it's easier to tell you what I don't believe in than what I do. Perhaps my nickname is as a good an indication as any.'

They withdrew to the sitting room where 'Zen' placed steaming cups of herbal tea on the tables that were still called 'coffee tables' though coffee no longer existed. Gilchrist picked up the record that Zen had removed from the machine, and idly glanced at it. Mozart, indeed. His 44th Symphony, K.705, composed in the year 1793. Gilchrist gazed at this perfectly ordinary and familiar object open-mouthed. He felt a sense of vertigo. 1793? He must have been mistaken, but he could have sworn . . . Or was this some complicated joke on the part of Zaleski? For a moment the world around him was blotted out. It was as if he were sitting in some desert place, hearing nothing, seeing nothing except the record sleeve with its absurd legend.

'Assynt – indeed the whole of the Highlands – are really an enormous sponge,' Zaleski was explaining. 'Even the mountains – they are either naked stone like Suilven, or simply vertical bogs, like Stac Polly. By the way, do you know how to pronounce *that* one?' and he pointed over his shoulder.

'No, not Quinn-ag,' he said laughing and bringing out what was evidently an ancient joke. 'Cognac, my dear, that's the pronunciation, the way the old Gaels used to say it. Considering that the Hebrides contain an island called Rum, it isn't very strange that Assynt contains a mountain pronounced Cognac. Not that either of those drinks exist any more.'

'Then why,' said Jenny, 'isn't there anywhere in Scotland named Whisky?'

'A good question. Have a wee dram.'

'Not for me,' said Gilchrist.

'*Slainte*,' said Jenny, 'And, forgive my curiosity, but that little figurine — it's very beautiful.'

'The Madonna and Child. It's a copy of the one that used to stand in Notre Dame, in Paris. The tenderness of motherhood, also, I sometimes think, the smile of divine wisdom. Lovely, isn't she?'

Very sexual too, thought Gilchrist.

'Then you're a Catholic?'

'Not I, my dear, though my Polish family was. She is here for her beauty, and because she belonged to my grandfather.'

'Do you go to church?'

'No. You see, I don't think God does either.

'But you're very silent, Gilchrist. Visiting one of your alternative worlds, I'll be bound.'

'Yes,' said Gilchrist, returning with a jolt to the present moment. 'Yes, that's exactly . . .' He replaced the record sleeve on its table, meanwhile watching the old man narrowly to see if, by any chance, he could descry some hint of amusement on his face at the success of his practical joke. Nothing.

And at once he knew that, when he returned to Edinburgh and looked up the biographies of Wolfgang Amadeus Mozart, he would find that the composer had not died of typhus (or perhaps been poisoned by Salieri) in the year 1791, but had lived instead to a ripe old age; and that there would be no way of showing what had once, in some other world, been true. Now his initial amazement had passed, he decided that this constituted an additional proof of the truth of his theory. Or rather, there was no proof, and in the nature of things could be none. When had he shifted into this other world, where Mozart had not died in 1791? No doubt at that moment on the pavement in Heriot Row, when the carriage wheel had veered aside.

He suddenly realised that 'Zen' was addressing him a question. 'I'm sorry, my mind was wandering.'

The old man repeated his inquiry, and Gilchrist drew breath, cautiously sipped at his soda, and imposed on his audience of two a brief but dramatic silence into which all his meditations of the past month were linked and united, like the fragments of a puzzle automatically finding their proper place in his thoughts.

'First let me ask you this. Do you accept that there are indeed alternative worlds, that they are all continually splitting off from ours, and that ours is but one of them?'

Zen shook his head. 'You cannot catch me like that. I accept that it is . . . a scientific possibility. But isn't the solution to evil given already by the Christian churches?'

'You mean that whatever nasty things may happen to us in this life, we shall all be well rewarded in heaven?'

'Exactly.'

'Does that convince you?'

'Frankly no, but then I am not a Christian. I am not even a Catholic.' He smiled wrily.

'Why does it not convince you?'

'Well, for all the reasons that have been discussed since time began. Remember Dostoevsky's tale (I repeat it from memory, for it's years since I read it). Once there was a 10-year-old boy, the only son of a widowed peasant woman, who took it into his head to steal some flowers for his mother from a nobleman's garden. The noble asked him if he were the guilty one, and he replied he was, with the frankness of a child. Then the noble bound his hands behind his back, called up his wolf-hounds and his henchmen, and went down into the village. The villagers were brought in from the fields to watch, and the child's mother wept for fear and fell upon her knees begging his lordship for her child's life. He spurned her with his foot, and commanded the boy to be stripped naked. Then he advised him to run as fast he could, while he set his hounds on him. And there, in the midst of the village, the child was torn to pieces in front of his mother's eyes.

79

She, it is reported, wept so much that afterwards she could never see again.

'Now let me ask you what could atone for that woman's suffering? Eternity? Was her suffering then not *real*? Did it never happen? Was it expunged from the record of history? You cannot answer the problem of evil by saying it is *paid for*. Can you pay a mother for the death of her child?

'Why, Dostoevsky has a conclusive argument. Imagine if you like that *you*, Jenny, were the architect of the world. Imagine that you had to start the world going, kick it on its course, fix the stars in the heavens, wind up the hearts of men and start them ticking. Imagine that it was necessary, to make everything turn out all right in the end, that one little child should suffer torment, excruciating torment all its life long. Would you consent to be the world's architect, if that were the condition?'

Jenny was silent. Then she shook her head.

'If you are doubtful, if you shake your head, then you must have more goodness in your heart than the Christian god. Think what a terrible dilemma must have confronted Him when He created the world. Not merely one child was to suffer, but millions upon uncountable millions, for thousands upon thousands of years. And along with them uncountable millions of adults, and along with them the beasts of the fields, the birds of the air, the creatures in the depths of the ocean.

'In short,' said Zaleski, turning to Gilchrist, 'I admit the problem of evil. But I fail to see how you can answer it by your talk of alternative worlds. Surely they would create ... merely *more* evil!'

'Well,' said Gilchrist, 'let us see how the argument goes. First you must remember that, as I was saying the other day, if two paths present themselves and consciousness appears only on one of them, then that consciousness will not perceive death as occurring, but *must* take the path of survival.'

'All right,' said Zaleski.

'So in cases like that, the problem of evil is solved.'

'Well ...' began the old man.

'Secondly,' said Gilchrist, ignoring him, 'the sorrow of the mother at the death of her son is instantly allayed by the doctrine

80

of the Branching Paths, because she would know that, in other worlds, in Ifwhere, as I call it, her son would infallibly survive. Thus, when I realised at last the truth of things, my grief for my wife was — not healed — but soothed, because I knew that, in Ifwhere, she must be alive and happy. And I said to myself, the condition of my own survival in this world must be her death — for why else would God have inflicted such pain upon me?'

'I see,' said Zaleski. 'Then do you suppose that, in Ifwhere, the Scots are not the sole survivors of the Holocaust — and indeed that in some of the worlds of Ifwhere the Holocaust never occurred?'

'No doubt. In some of those other worlds, the Bolshevik *coup d'état* of 1917 never took place. In some of them, Mozart died in 1791. In some of them, Napoleon was never born.'

'And in 1179, I suppose you will say, the Normans were defeated by an English rebellion, and banished from these shores. In which case, we would all still be speaking Anglo-Saxon.'

'But how,' continued Zen, 'does this solve the problem of evil? You must admit that, even in a world where the family of Harold Godwinson was restored to the English throne, suffering must still occur.'

'We have to suffer a little,' said Gilchrist, 'in order to avoid greater suffering. It is the law of life, it is what prevents children putting their hand into the fire.'

There was a thunderstruck silence. The old man stared at Gilchrist for, it seemed, a full minute, as if, white hair and all, he had been turned to stone by a thought.

'Do you mean that — I hardly dare suggest it — You cannot surely mean that, in your theory, each consciousness, each soul explores the path before him and ... avoids entering upon paths of evil and suffering?'

Gilchrist nodded silently.

'But what then of those who *do* suffer? Are they, according to your view of things, no longer *real?*' The old man sounded shocked, appalled.

'They are deceptive shadows thrown out of that further dimension, out of Ifwhere, and appearing in Herenow in distorted and suffering form. For,' explained Gilchrist in the very tones of quiet reason, 'this is the only way to preserve the innocence of God.'

'And so, you mean, it must be so? Well,' said Zaleski, turning to Jenny, 'what do you think of all this, my dear?'

'Och, I've heard it all before,' said Jenny. 'It's an *active* idea, don't you think?'

'And what are you going to do with your idea? Stop, don't tell me, for I know what people do with ideas these days. Found a church.'

'Wish me luck,' said Gilchrist, looking, in the golden lamplight, like a smiling statue, a parody of the Buddha, divinely calm and confident.

'Rimmon has helped you and will help you again. These four weeks, I assume, have been no holiday, but a means of checking your views against my rather rusty knowledge, and of planning your next steps. Rimmon is a man of substance.'

'A man of character too,' said Jenny, wondering why she nevertheless so disliked him.

'Men of character are usually men of bad character. Do you want some advice?'

Gilchrist looked at him in silence.

'I owe it to you whether you want it or not. It is this. Your idea is brilliant, perhaps a little too brilliant. But do not make a doctrine. It always goes wrong. Let me remind you what superstition is. It is religion taken literally. All creeds are, properly understood, merely metaphors. Even she,' he added, pointing to the Madonna. 'The Christians made a doctrine out of divine love, and they ended up with the Inquisition. Zen made a doctrine out of not making a doctrine, and even that went wrong, for it became the creed of the Samurai, that warrior caste whose swords were of the sharpest tempered steel. Do you know the story?'

They shook their heads.

'I promise you it is true. A Samurai sword was not a good one unless it could cleave a man in two, from his left shoulder to his right thigh. So before a sword could be used, it had to be tested. The Samurai would therefore lie in wait at some crossroads and await the passing of some peaceful peasant going home with his shovel over his shoulder. Then ... But "peasants are merely

82

peasants, and nothing matters because good and evil are one, and all will be well in the end."

'Make a doctrine, and you turn God into the devil.'

Gilchrist was astonished, indignant. 'But I cannot keep silent! Men need hope, they need the mercy of God. Would you withhold bread from a starving child?'

Gilchrist and the old man began to argue, at first in the tones of calm discussion, but soon in accents of genuine bitterness. Bitterness at least on Gilchrist's side, for Zaleski's voice, no matter what he said, remained dispassionate — which made things worse. Jenny tried several times to intervene, but it was useless. At last she rose decisively and announced that it was late, that dinner had been 'thermo-nuclear' and 'a real melt-down', but that really they must leave now.

'That nice old man,' she reproached Gilchrist on the doorstep. 'Did you have to be so nasty to him?'

'There's nothing annoys me so much,' he replied, 'as stubborn folk who stare facts in the face and won't see them.'

She felt uneasy for a moment, almost wondering if she had made the right commitment. But she was at that early stage of affection when one is tempted to believe that one's beloved is always right. Later, she was sure, she would have no doubts at all. Nonetheless, she remembered the old physicist's last words. He had turned to point up to the little figure of the Madonna, slender, archly curvaceous on her pedestal, smiling inscrutably down at her child, and had said:

'Do you know why she smiles? She smiles because she is eternal, and what she can see in the future causes her to smile in the present.'

9

'T Ain't No Sin

*Can a man take fire in his
bosom, and his clothes not
be burned?*

PROVERBS 6:27

Perth, Thursday 18 June 2037

Twilight, but the atmosphere was still close and oppressive. The
grass of Perth's South Inch Park, fifteen acres between river and
city, was invisible, covered by an impatient, restless multitude.
The lofty trees, formed up like troops of grenadiers, boxed the
throng into vast regimental squares. A loudspeaker lurked in
every sixth tree. The impatience of each man, woman and child
was locked away inside his head, each head locked away in turn
inside its plastic helmet. All the more impatient for this double
prison. At the side of the road, two more figures keeled over. It
was a hot evening for radsuits and, hidden in his tent at the rear of
the platform, Gilchrist, on his knees, was thanking Jesus for the
continuing heatwave. Eight weeks already, ever more sultry, and
what a godsend for his evangelical crusade!

When the crusade had commenced twelve weeks ago at
Berwick and Kelso, it had drizzled gently upon them; at Jedburgh
and Galashiels it had been merely overcast. But since then,
through the Borders, Dumfries and Galloway, through Ayrshire
and the satellite towns of New Rome, 'How generous the grace of
the Lord had been!'

For a tent, however enormous, would not do. It was essential
for the full effectiveness of the message that meetings be held in
the open air.

Gilchrist genuflected once more before the image of Christ,
hanging crucified from a tent pole. Wearing (like the Saviour's
image) only underpants, he stepped to the spyhole at the back of
the platform, from where he could estimate the size of the crowd,

supervise the proceedings, judge the pitch of excitement which had been reached. Already the voices of the singing, marching procession could be heard as it wound its way through the streets of Perth behind them — and the crowd held their breaths, straining their ears to listen to that distant, sacramental music. At the end of the street opening, half a mile away, the first glitter of the candles appeared, one held in the hand of each celebrant, and Gilchrist, signing to his helpers, had the floodlights instantly doused, so that the whole vast field was plunged into an alarming blackness. The singing swelled, the procession of candles ceremoniously approached, a cortège of lights hovering five feet in the air as if under supernatural command. The waiting audience too began to join in the words of the song, hypnotic, verse after verse, singing of a light in darkness.

As the procession swung to a slow halt, lined up five hundred candles long between the ranks of the waiting citizens of Perth, Gilchrist's Choir of Angels struck up the theme music of The Branching Wynd:

The branching wynd,

Bound to follow the branching wynd,

Where the wind blows,

The winding track goes . . .

and so on. The words, as Gilchrist was aware, were hardly great poetry, but the divine message had had no time to wait upon the vagaries of inspiration. Effectiveness was what counted. The tune had a plangent catchiness, and the Sacred Band (the Soulwarmers, he liked to call them) were rocking and swinging like a record from the 1930s, with that subtle and compelling lilt that set people's feet unconsciously moving, so that they began willy-nilly to sway in unison.

In one of the other tents behind the stand, Archie Rimmon and Virgil Appelbaum were looking on too through a discreetly raised flap.

'Jenny's not here tonight.'

'She's back in Edinburgh,' explained Rimmon, 'pregnant with the heir of prophecy. Did I tell you Helen is too?' he added with pride. 'My third!'

Virgil, impressed by all this fertility, giggled foolishly and

85

offered his congratulations. '*Allegretto*! But you − ' He began to stutter with embarrassment. − 'your post in the Cult . . .'

'That's why I brought you here this evening. I'm resigning my job at Von Däniken's. I've been "converted".'

A few lights flicked on here and there in the trees like distant stars. Above the audience arc lights flashed and died, leaving a deeper darkness after them. To the accompaniment of tense, spaced-out chords held above an ominous rhythm of drums, Gilchrist's cheer-leader intoned the description of the Earth's destruction as it is written in the Apocalypse of John:

'And I beheld . . .'

'And I beheld,' murmured the audience.

'When he had opened the sixth seal,'

' . . . the sixth seal,' they chanted.

'And lo, there was a great earthquake.'

'And lo,' roared the throng, itself like an earthquake.

There was a crashing of music, a glare of lights succeeded by darkness. A wind of fear blew through the crowd, and Gilchrist (who during these last exchanges had hastily struggled into his radsuit) stepped out onto the platform. Since the lights all went on together at that moment, blinding the crowd, it was as if he had suddenly materialised in front of them. There was a moment's dazzled silence, then, as they perceived that the apparition wore the black and white radsuit of the Saviour, with its design of a branching tree, there was a brief roar of applause. This was cut short, choked off in mid-roar, whether because people felt that it was half blasphemous to applaud − or whether because they felt a burning eagerness to hear his words − who could say?

Gilchrist began to speak.

His words were carried, ringing and awesome, across the great park by microphones. To the north of the park, the serried grey stone terraces were battered and assaulted by the sound. It rang back from them like the trumpets of the angels who, on the Last Day, shall stand at the four corners of the Earth.

'After all,' said Rimmon to Virgil, 'I was in this from the start. That evening in Heriot Row, the moment of the New Revelation . . .'

'I remember it.'

'And who do you suppose has done all the organising that a spectacle like this requires? Wheedled the financiers, twisted the levers of industry, pulled golden strings in high places?'

'But the power of Gilchrist's message . . .'

'Of course,' said Rimmon. 'That too is my contribution to the cause.'

Gilchrist was describing the Holocaust in all its horror, enumerating the sufferings of mankind from blast, from firestorm, from radiation sickness, from famine, from mutation. Then he described the present day, the shortening of life, the misfortunes of the mutants, the barrenness of childless mothers, the sicknesses and suicides.

'For man is evil. We are sinners, aye, all sinners.'

The crowd groaned at the knowledge.

'But no, not only man is evil, but God is evil too. Ask yourselves — you, you, aye, each one of you — look each of you separately into your hearts and answer this. Suppose that God Himself comes to you and offers you this task — to create a new, a better universe. Only there is one condition — mark it well! — one terrible condition. In payment for the happiness of this new world of peace and beauty, one innocent bairn must suffer, must undergo the most appalling agonies . . .'

And Gilchrist repeated the dilemma of Dostoyevsky, as it had been told him by Zen Zaleski, fifteen months before. He added to it further tales of despair, and pointed at last the finger of accusation at God Himself, raising both his arms to the black night sky and calling on God to strike him dead.

'A consummate preacher,' Rimmon was saying appraisingly. 'Well, we all have undreamed-of talents. But you must admit the power of the stage setting. At night folk are at their most suggestible, Hitler knew that. This combination of lights and darkness, of drums and catchy tunes. But most of all — I must say I admire the way in which he threatens them with Hell — with Hell on earth — and drags them down into darkness, into the very pit of desperation. First he frightens them, that is the secret.'

'Frightens them?'

87

'Yes, it is beautifully done. He reveals to them the anger which they all, deep in their hearts, unconsciously feel. It is unconscious because they dread it, because it is an anger against God Himself. Moreover, it is justified, and they know it to be so! Yet they feel guilty experiencing that anger, and also terrified, because, without God, what hope is left to them? Oh, a wonderfully subtle recipe — blasphemy and faith, anger and fear, the truth of guilt revealed, all seething together in the same magic cauldron.'

Thunder growled far off (for it was a sultry night) and there were distant flashes of lightning on the horizon, but no thunderbolt came blasting down to knock the preacher off his perch. The lights had been dimming again all this while, and by now — save for the illuminated figure of Gilchrist blaspheming on his platform — the darkness was absolute. Many of the congregation were on their knees, others were weeping; an infection of grief and terror overwhelmed them as if they were a single consciousness, and that consciousness were held in Gilchrist's grip like a sparrow — to be crushed to death if he willed it.

Then he offered them hope. The promise of the Branching Paths poured from him like a certainty. The lights came slowly on again, subtly coloured so it was like a dawn rising from the very soil they stood on. The preacher had removed his helmet, and those at the front of the audience could see that his face was streaming with tears.

And now came the final clinching moment of his preaching. 'Our Lord Jesus Christ said to the crippled man — a mutant of those days in distant Palestine — "Take up thy bed and walk" and the man took up his bed and walked, for he was healed. Never again did he limp, never again ...

'Now I say unto you — as that was a sign of healing in far-off Palestine, so let this be a sign of healing here today on the grassy turf of Scotland — *Cast off your radsuits and be free!*'

'Megadeath!' babbled Virgil unhappily from his tent-flap, and clutched at the throat of his zip-fasteners as if someone were about to leap upon him and tear the garment off — the peak of indecency!

Rimmon regarded him ironically. 'I'm afraid if you really intend to be born again and see the light, you'll just have to take it off like everyone else.'

'But why?' protested Virgil. 'Why such an − obscene − embarrassing − ?'

In the park outside, in the open spaces, under the trees, at the foot of the preacher's rostrum, people were shouting and singing as they ripped and tore at their oversuits with a haste that popped zip-fasteners and sent buttons flying. Freedom! Salvation! The branching paths! The lights blazed down on a scene of enthusiasm and chaos such as Perth, perhaps, had never witnessed. One man, now that his outer covering was gone, revealed to be a short-armed mutant, was crouching on the grass and barking like a dog. Young men and girls, old ladies and gentlemen from before the Holocaust, embraced at random, tears of joy streaming down their faces. A few shamefaced individuals, less suggestible than their fellow-citizens, crept furtively away, feeling inadequate at not being able to express their feelings so outrageously. Several people, particularly near Gilchrist's rostrum, fell on the ground frothing at the mouth, shrieking, the whites of their eyes showing. Truth! Revelation! The Holy Ghost descends!

'It's very simple,' Rimmon was explaining. 'To remove your radsuit is a sure sign of your adherence to the Kirk. It divides group from group in the most spectacular way. It is all the *better* if going about "half naked" worries and embarrasses you, for then you wear your adherence painfully (or rather you undress it painfully) and are confirmed in that adherence with every mortified step you take. Yet at the same time this badge of shame converts into pride, into a provocation against the suited. You know how the suited feel about you − shocked, disgusted! − because you too feel shocked at yourself. By an effort of will you have risen above all that, into freedom, into a divine region, beyond shame. You are for evermore assured of your own rectitude.'

As the evening was close and the clothes people wore under their oversuits were scanty, there was a quite shocking number of bare arms and legs − and even bare chests − now exposed

89

upon the Park. Whistles began to blow, and the police in their checkered black and white radsuits began running to and fro, shouting commands and making scores of arrests.

'Active!' said Rimmon. 'Persecution is an excellent boost for a sect!'

The police, however, soon had a much more serious problem. Discarded oversuits were being hauled into piles, and the piles set alight. Bonfires of clothing blazed in every corner of the Park, and the populace danced around them like cannibals at a corroboree. A rhythmic clapping broke out to the words of a popular hymn, and eightsome reels were soon being danced to its tune.

'You mustn't suppose that young lassie is pretending,' said Rimmon, pointing down to the foot of the rostrum, where a girl was having what appeared to be an epileptic fit. 'No, it seems that the Holy Spirit takes some people this way. It has been described to me as the sensation of a *white darkness* creeping up through the limbs and overwhelming the mind. It seems it is quite irresistible, and perfectly natural. Possession. Divine Grace. You have heard of the Quakers, of course.'

Meanwhile, the Band was playing, Gilchrist was on his knees on the rostrum thanking God that Heaven's grace had been extended to its poor benighted sheep, and the Superintendent of Police could be seen, grossly indecent in shirt and trousers, holding a long tree branch and forking his own black and white checked radsuit into the flames.

'B-but he of all people,' stammered Virgil. '*C-con fuego!*'

'Surprising, isn't it?' said Rimmon as if nothing ever surprised him. 'Do you not remember the story of St Paul? Sometimes it's those who resist the Saviour most passionately, whom He most passionately overwhelms. Emotion builds and builds, then suddenly its flames blow back in the opposite direction!

'There is only one thing this new religion lacks,' he added thoughtfully.

'And what is that?' asked Virgil, still clutching his radsuit by the throat as if he feared it would throttle him — or perhaps tear *itself* off.

'Nothing very much,' replied Rimmon, removing his helmet

90

and then unzipping himself to reveal a respectable (but feather-light) twentieth-century style suit below it. 'I'm sure we'll be able to add it.

'In the Lord's good time.'

He stepped out of his superclothes.

10

Ole Miss

The rod and reproof give wisdom;
but a child left to himself
bringeth his mother to shame.

———— PROVERBS 29:15 ————

Edinburgh, Friday 19 June 2037

With her taut young muscles, Jenny was not as yet visibly pregnant, save when she undressed. Nonetheless, the Holy Federal Kirks of Scotland paid a generous wage to expectant mothers from the third month on, and she could well have retired from teaching, supported Gilchrist, moved to a bigger flat and begun furnishing it on the proceeds.

Only they had flitted to a bigger flat already, for Rimmon's wealthy backers had enabled them to cash some of their expectations in advance. Besides, the Crusade was going well, she heard — crowds flocking to hear Peter from every quarter of Scotland, and thousands being saved nightly — just like Our Redeemer in the New Testament! Clearly they would soon be, mm, 'comfortably off'.

But she loved teaching. She loved her children, and most of all — she admitted it quite freely — that difficult class of thirteen 15-year-olds, containing Corinthia MacAndrew, Susan Mears, Karen Mackenzie and the rest. It would be with mixed feelings that, at the end of term on 2 July, she would say goodbye to them all for the last time and retire to her future career of pregnancy and motherhood. Of course, to be a mother would be wonderful, and it was such a privilege to be one of the 30 per cent who could. From her seat among the staff on the platform she cast a fond eye over the school assembly hall, trying to see if some of her favourite Lower Fourths were there tonight with their parents — Corinthia? Fiona? Christine?

92

What a pity the weather had broken tonight, though. The heatwave had been building up to this all the past month, and it was an evening of wind and pouring rain, not fit to let a mutant out in. Still, perhaps it wasn't raining in Perth.

The school orchestra and choir had by now all settled in their places and Mrs Mairi McInnes the headmistress rose to her feet, coughing for attention.

'Ladies and gentlemen, we're delighted to welcome you here tonight on such a *bad* night, and we just hope that at the end of the evening you'll think it was all worthwhile. We think you may be quite surprised by the accomplishments of our children. They've worked so hard and put in such a lot of effort, and I'm sure you'll all recognise this when you hear them. I know we have a marvellous lot of parents in this school, and they back us up so generously, and we do hope, when you hear the results of all their hard work, you'll realise just how very important parental support can be . . .'

And so on. Jenny gritted her teeth and thought how like Mrs McInnes this speech was, and just how much it revealed about her. Well, this was one reason why she wasn't sorry to be leaving in ten days' time.

The school concert began, and Jenny relaxed. It was true the violins were out of tune, but then they always were, weren't they? And the children sang and played with such vigour. Perhaps indeed, safely inoculated by their music teacher's enthusiasm, they hadn't heard Mrs McInnes's words. The hour passed all too quickly, and it was with surprise that she heard the symphony of coughs, of scraping chairs, clattering umbrellas and chatter that marked the end of the concert. The clumping of boots, the rustling and zipping of five hundred radsuits being donned. Jenny felt the pressure of a gentle hand upon her wrist.

'Jenny dear,' said Mrs McInnes, 'could I have a little word with you? Just five minutes of your time. Perhaps if you could come to my room.' A kindly smile accompanied these words.

Oh dear, thought Jenny to herself. But what can she do to me? I've only ten days left.

'Now this is really very distressing for me to have to say,' said the headmistress, once the door of her room had been carefully

93

closed, the shutters drawn, and when she had gone a second time to the door, opening it and peering out as if she expected to find someone in the corridor outside with his ear to the keyhole.

'Really very distressing, but I'm sure you'll agree yourself, my dear, that I really have no alternative. You realise we're a Kirk foundation, and the governors leave me no alternative.'

Jenny wished she could stop repeating the word 'alternative'.

'I know you had a difficult start in the school, my dear, and that awful Lower Fourth class really made things difficult for you – no interest in their work, no interest in anything, I sometimes think, except making trouble. The only one who shows any moral sense at all is my own daughter Aileen. It's a terrible thing to say and makes me sound prejudiced, I know, but I do try to be as objective as possible. I suppose it was rather naughty of me giving them such an inexperienced teacher. But really, I did think that by this time you might have learnt how to handle them.

'But what is this I hear?' She paused dramatically as if expecting Jenny to reply.

'I'm sure I don't know, Mrs McInnes.'

'Well, that won't do at all, Jenny, and is not very honest of you, if you'll allow me to say so. You can't pretend that you are not aware of what you have been teaching these poor children in their catechism class these past few months. What, telling them the doctrines of all the different kirks? I don't know whether you realise how careful one has to be with young minds. They mustn't be *stretched* too much, you mustn't make too much *demand* on their abilities. But worst of all, I hear you have been explaining the beliefs of the Str – I mean the Kirk of Instant Salvation.'

There was a pause while Mrs McInnes watched Jenny's lips carefully as if she expected a miraculous toad to pop from between them, as from the mouth of the wicked daughter in the fairy-tale.

'But I *am* a Salvationist,' protested Jenny. 'My husband . . .'

'Yes, I know, dear, but here you are employed by the Auld Kirk, and . . .'

'I was only answering the children's questions,' said Jenny weakly.

'Answering their questions! Dear me, you have to be very

94

careful with children's questions, as I know to my own cost with my own daughter. I am told, for example — though I shall not say by whom — that you have been telling the bairns that the sun, moon and stars were not made in a day. Now where have you picked that up, my dear? Certainly not in the Bible!'

Supposing that God just waved his wand, thought Jenny. Like pressing an electric switch. It's a way of avoiding a sense of wonder.

'But there is worse, much worse.' The headmistress paused for effect. 'You have been seen these past few days coming into school — I hardly like to pronounce the word but there is no point in beating about the bush — undressed!' Mrs McInnes pronounced this final word lingeringly and with emphasis. She went on:

'Now I distinctly remember, my dear — and you yourself as a straightforward young person will confirm this — telling you four weeks ago that, no matter what your personal beliefs may be, here you are employed by the Auld Kirk, and it is simply not permissible for the staff of a dignified and ancient foundation like ours to come to school in a state of undress.'

'I was wearing indoor clothes. It's a question of my religious faith, Mrs McInnes. My husband . . .'

'Jenny, Jenny,' said Mrs McInnes shaking her head in sorrow, 'I know it is difficult for you, and I know your husband must have certain expectations of you, but I am sure that you yourself realise, in your heart of hearts, if you only looked into your conscience at some quiet moment, that *it is simply not right.*

'I am therefore banning you — and it is for your own good, my dear — banning you from setting foot in this school again. You will take your wages — ' the headmistress produced an envelope from behind her back ' — and you will leave the premises tonight, and we shall simply all of us hope that your pregnancy continues to go so well.'

'But my class,' said Jenny. 'Can't I say goodbye to my class?'

'I'm sure you will realise, Jenny, that it is much better for all concerned if you do not.'

Jenny wished that Mrs McInnes was not so thirled to the words

95

'realise' and 'simply'. Aloud, she said: 'I just want to see them for one last time. I'm . . . I'm fond of them.'

'This is very painful for me too, Jenny,' said the headmistress. She added in tones of absolute sincerity: 'No hard feelings, I hope.'

Jenny was aware that her face was wet. Perhaps they were tears of anger for, as she touched the polished brass handle of the door, she felt impelled to turn round and confront Mrs McInnes.

For the first time she looked her straight in the eye — though this was hard, because the headmistress was still keeping her slightly appalled gaze on Jenny's lips. 'That was a horrible way to do it!' said Jenny through her tears. 'Couldn't you have managed it differently?'

'Differently?' said Mrs McInnes, gazing at her with incomprehension.

11

There'll Be Some Changes Made

Speak, Lord; for thy servant heareth.

———— I SAMUEL 3:10 ————

July 2037 — September 2038

The Kirk of Instant Salvation set up their tents in Dundee, Aberdeen, Forfar, Arbroath, Kinross and Stirling. Jenny went with them for, the moment she had been dismissed, she had caught the electrobus to Perth, to weep on Peter's shoulder, to be comforted, and to help him in his divine ministry. When autumn came, the whole enormous travelling circus returned in triumph home to the capital where Gilchrist had not yet preached. He remembered the saying 'A prophet hath no honour in his own country', and he was determined that this prophet would.

Jenny felt, not exactly worried, but less totally contented, than she had at the outset of her joining Peter. There was nothing she could put her finger on. It was true she was beginning to get fat, but Peter was just as attentive as ever. Perhaps she was concerned about the flocks of young women who surrounded him, following him adoringly with their eyes, waiting for crumbs and kind words to fall from the master's table. If they had had tails they would have wagged them. Particularly those who belonged to the Kirk's official Choir of Angels. Their souls were no doubt immaculately saved, and their voices were certainly divine; but so were their faces and figures. Peter had splendid qualities, she knew, and she was a very lucky young woman, but he did rather bask in female adulation.

Surely there was nothing to worry about. He was a very busy man, conferring with his ministers, planning the next campaign, composing new hymns, new sermons, even finding time to take small classes of the newly saved, every moment of the day that he was not upon the rostrum thundering out dreadful reminders about the fire from heaven, and offering the heady wine of branching certainty.

There is a long tradition of calling new cults by uncomplimentary names. The Shakers, the Quakers, the Ranters, the Holy Rollers ... It was inevitable that Gilchrist's new religion should be nicknamed the Strippers. The sobriquet, however, suggests the wrong image. It was not for this reason that, on 12 August 2037, the Holy Federal Parliament of the Kirks of Scotland in solemn conclave declared that 'the removal in public and in the open air by any person or persons of any item of the outer garb or raiment of that same person or persons, commonly called the radsuit, oversuit or superclothing, shall henceforth and by these presents be illegal and punishable by the full rigour of the Law'.

No, it was not from any disapproval of indecency that the assembled Kirks pronounced this judgement, but because they feared for their own congregations. A 30 per cent falling off in church attendance, worse in some of the more arthritic communions. It was already clear that the new Kirk of Instant Salvation (ridiculous name!) would have to be represented in the next Parliament — but this was what worried them, how strongly would it have to be represented?

For Gilchrist's new Kirk was consummately well organised. In every town, every city, every hamlet out of which his circus rolled, he left behind a network of 'tabernacles', little study groups of twelve new converts. The deacon of each tabernacle went round personally once a week to the homes of these converts, chatting to them watchfully, addressing himself to their problems, advising them 'which path to take'. In addition to the weekly prayer meeting, there was a weekly meeting of study, where the tenets and teachings of the new Kirk were carefully expounded, and any doubts resolved. The neophyte was expected to commit effort and time to bringing new converts to the Kirk. In return, he could feel that he instantly 'belonged', that he was cared for, that he was part of a great and growing community.

The Prophet's success in Edinburgh was as spectacular as it had been in Forfar and Aberdeen. The citizens of the capital were flattered by being treated as sophisticates — by his references to diabolic works, to saints of Satanism such as Bohr, Planck, Einstein, Feynman, Rutherford and Oppenheimer. At last, they said to each other, at last a religion that a thinking person can adopt.

The charge of Devil worship levelled at Gilchrist by his opponents in the other, threatened Kirks, was a treacherous and slippery weapon which could turn in its user's hand. The Black Arts of Science were feared and dreaded, but for that very reason held a terrifying prestige, as anything that is feared for its power will do. And that power had been real. No one who looked round him at the devastated Earth could doubt that. By contrast, what signs were there of the power of God? In short, if supernatural power was what you sought, you would find it in the occult arts of Beelzebub rather than the sunny hopes of the kirks. Here was a new faith that promised to reconcile the power of the Devil with the optimistic messages of the Christian God. The more anathemas his opponents pronounced against Gilchrist, the more people flocked to hear him.

As for the new prohibition upon 'stripping', this was a dead letter even before it had been promulgated. What could the police do when nine out of ten thousand attenders at the same meeting tore off their radsuits and burnt them? Was it sufficient to arrest ten culprits, twenty, or even thirty? Besides, the new federal law would not stand up. It was solemnly handed down as an opinion at the High Court in Parliament Square that 'only the *removal* of the oversuit is reprehensible. To be already without it is not forbidden by the law. The actual *act* of removal has therefore to be witnessed'.

Parliament went back to the statute books, but it was too late. There were by this time simply too many Instant Salvationists. On the morning the new law was due to be passed, the High Street, George IV Bridge, the Mound, Johnstone Terrace and all the nearby roads were blocked by thousands of Strippers, holding banners and chanting; and the reverend but intimidated members of the Parliament threw the bill out.

The Kirk swelled, and so did Jenny and her bosom friend Helen. In November they both produced beautiful bouncing girl babies.

Early in the New Year Gilchrist took his crusade to New Rome. He had left that city almost till last because it had always been such a hard nut for theatrical performers to crack.

This new Eternal City, a replacement for the one destroyed near Ostia in Italy, contained at the time three separate Popes, named Pius XIII, Innocent XIV and Benevolent I. There was, of course, another Pope Pius XIII in Hobart, Tasmania, but the three had not as yet made contact with him, for they recognised neither his existence nor, indeed, that of each other. The impending arrival of Gilchrist, his cheer-leaders, his Choir of Angels and his Sacred Band of Soulwarmers, at last drove the three Popes into one room together.

The meeting took place on neutral ground, a fine nineteenth-century panelled chamber in the old Glasgow City Hall. A special triangular table had been found for the occasion, so that each Supreme Pontiff was in a position of absolute equality *vis-à-vis* the others; and a third door was opened in one of the walls so that no Pope would have to tread in another's footsteps.

The first day began well, with one of those pieces of harmless irreverence which priests find so hilarious.

'I wondered if we'd be wearing haloes of different colours,' joked Innocent, 'but I see we've left them at home.'

His colleagues tittered at this sally, embraced each other warily, and sat down.

'An ideal table for our confabulations,' said Benevolent. 'A symbol of the Trinity.'

They all laughed comfortably.

'Which of us is the Holy Spirit?' asked Innocent, and they all laughed again, a little louder.

'And which the Holy Father?' asked Pius. There was a frozen silence.

Benevolent restored harmony by switching the conversation to their enemy the Antichrist, whom he called 'Peter Prophet' and 'the Irreverent Gilchrist'. Loud clerical chuckles broke out again, and the three Popes spent an enjoyable half hour tearing the doctrines of the Strippers to pieces.

'Do you realise,' said Pius, 'what this abominable creed implies? When Christ comes again, He'll come in fifty different ways, in a hundred different guises. Perhaps He'll even be preaching a hundred different messages.'

'Heresy,' they agreed.

'This doctrine is absurd,' said Innocent. 'It states that if anything can go right, it will. It's Murphy's Law turned on its head!'

There was a silence. Pius looked sharply at him: 'That was a quite uncalled-for remark.'

Innocent bethought himself, a moment too late, that Pius XIII's surname had been Murphy. He had been guilty of *lèse-papauté*.

From that moment things went from bad to worse. The rest of the day was spent in trying to decide which of the three was the true Pope; but since this would have meant the other two being considered as Antipopes, the discussion came to nothing.

On the second day they attempted to resolve their differences by discussing doctrinal matters. Pius declared that he was the true Vicar of Christ because his Church insisted on priestly celibacy, whereas that of Innocent turned a blind eye to their sexual peccadilloes, and that of Benevolent committed the even less canonical offence of permitting its priests to marry. To this Innocent and Benevolent protested that they were both just as infallible as Pius; Innocent spoke sweetly of divine pardon for the weakness of the flesh; and Benevolent pointed out how vital it was that Holy Church should reproduce herself. He also made the mistake of letting fall the word 'hypocrisy', which caused the second day's meeting to close in uproar, in the course of which his lofty white tiara was snatched from his head and stamped upon. Worse still, his rivals stamped on each other's feet in doing so.

This was Schism indeed! The three Holy Fathers departed to their respective Vaticans and never spoke to each other again; and New Rome was now a *città aperta*, helpless before the coming evangelist onslaught.

But perhaps the most spectacular episode in the new Kirk's expanding power – certainly the one that brought at the time the most adherents — occurred on the evening of 30 January at New Rome's proud auditorium, the Kelvin Hall.

A special stage had been built for the occasion, all the seats had been cleared from the stalls, and the hall was packed with radsuits, which people had refrained from taking off at the door — for they were awaiting Gilchrist's signal, that spiritual climax when they would shed their old beliefs along with their clothing, as a light from heaven shone into their hearts.

Meanwhile, such illumination was still awaited, and the service had reached that dramatic point where all the lights were doused, save for an eerie red glow round Gilchrist's feet and for the flashing of artificial lightning from the ceiling a hundred feet above their heads. From the darkness of the stage before them, Gilchrist's voice was intoning terrifying blasphemies — how Christ had been crucified for His own sin in creating an evil world, how that sacrifice was not enough, and how human children continued to perish every day of leukaemia by the will of their heavenly father. From time to time Gilchrist's tall figure could be glimpsed in a flash of lightning or in the crimson glimmer from about his feet, casting a sinister light upwards at his face. So that, as the frightened audience muttered to themselves, it was like having a vision of Satan himself.

Gilchrist's voice ceased in the middle of a sentence. A crash echoed from the darkened stage — a crash so deafening you might think the sky had fallen to punish the blasphemer. Then sounds of confusion could be heard — confused shouts, succeeded by the shrieking of terrified sopranos. The lights all flashed on together, and the audience, dazzled and bewildered by the glare, took a moment to make out what was happening.

It was a melodramatic scene. The only way onto the stage was from various doors at the back of it, but all these were blocked by the wailing lassies of the choir, who were scratching and clawing to get out. Meanwhile, male helpers were heaving and pushing to get in through the same doors. For a critical half a minute, it was stalemate.

In the middle of the platform stood two solitary figures facing each other, side on to the congregation. One of them was Gilchrist himself, his arms raised, not because he had surrendered, but because he had not had time to drop them after his imprecations to Jehovah. Four feet away from him stood a young man, dressed in black, pointing a gun at Gilchrist's midriff. At the front of the stage lay the microphone whose headlong fall had no doubt produced that ear-splitting crash.

'Now don't be silly,' said Gilchrist, lowering his arms cautiously, and reaching out his right hand as if to accept a present. 'Give me the gun.'

He had spoken calmly, but the young man's answering voice was shrill and anguished. 'In the name of the Moral Majority, I tell thee, Peter Gilchrist, thou art damned to all eternity as a blaspheming heathen.'

The Moral Majority was a tiny minority kirk, whose holiest sacrament was the burning of books. Homer, Sylvia Plath, Shakespeare, Enid Blyton, Hugh MacDiarmid. Any books except Burns and the Bible. They specialised in forcing their way, in true evangelical style, into people's houses and casting any books they found there out through the window. This particular zealot had an American accent. He must come from the Isle of Skye or thereabouts.

'I heard a still, small voice in the night. I obey the Lord's command,' cried the young man.

All this while the Choir of Angels, hitting notes much higher than they had been trained for, were struggling to get out. Their pretty faces were contorted with fear, their charming mouths all open pinkly on a shriek. The wreckage of one big white angel's wing had showered its feathers all around the stage, so that it looked like the snow in February 2036 in Heriot Row. No one could either enter or leave, for at the back of the stage it was still stalemate.

One old man in the circle, mistaking it all for a Wagner opera he had witnessed in his youth, rose to his feet and applauded.

Gilchrist collected himself and said, 'You cannot hurt me. If I die, it will be in Ifwhere. It cannot be in Herenow. Moreover, you cannot hurt yourself. The mercy of the Lord will preserve us both.'

'Thou art a liberal, a commie and a pervert,' clamoured his assailant, for he had been brought up according to the true faith of the New World (now the Old World), and still used an outdated vocabulary. As far as the congregation were concerned, he might as well have been talking Russian, or some other dead language.

'In one of the possible worlds at least,' Gilchrist said in tones of sweet reason, 'your gun will fail to go off. In another you will have forgotten to load it. In several others you will change your mind. Give it to me.'

'Yeah, I'll give it to thee,' said the young man. Audibly, his teeth were chattering.

All this had taken but a few seconds, though to Gilchrist it seemed like minutes. Deaf to the screaming of his choristers, he even had time to notice the calmness of his own mind. Could there be any more agonising test of his faith? Yet it stood solid as a rock. He remembered the arguments of Everett, and Virgil's strange tendency to 'shimmer'. He remembered Mozart's 44th Symphony. He remembered this same experience of time extended, drawn to a halt, hovering. He remembered the glitter of the thawing snow, the street lights reflected off wet cobblestones, the startled mare, the carriage wheel rolling towards his face, flashing like the Reaper's scythe. He knew he could not be killed, he knew that on one at least of the paths which reached forward from this moment his life was bound to continue. Life was a game of Russian roulette in which the player always won. He felt exceedingly pleased with himself.

Serenely, therefore, and as if this were happening in Ifwhere to some altogether different person, he watched the young man's lips trembling, the beads of sweat upon his forehead (it was hot under the arc lights), the wavering motion of the small black muzzle of the pistol, the shaking of the assassin's fingers as he took aim, braced himself and squeezed the trigger. These actions seemed slow, deliberate, distinct and separate, and all the while Gilchrist stood there watching, smiling gently to himself.

There was a feeble click from the revolver, and Gilchrist stepped forward and took it from the young man's outstretched hand. It had, as he predicted, failed to go off.

The proportion of converts that night at the Kelvin Hall was particularly high, and the rest of Gilchrist's crusade in New Rome was a triumph.

104

By the end of February, he was back in Edinburgh. Then it was the Borders again and, come Easter, the north-east coast, Buchan, Elgin and Nairn. From the region of the earthquake fault at Comrie and in the Great Glen, strange moving lights were reported, bowling like hoops over the roof-tops, and these were confidently believed to be a sign from Heaven. Gilchrist's entry into Inverness was like a Roman triumph, his return to the capital reminiscent of a coronation. At the elections in September 2038, the Salvationists took 30 per cent of the seats in the Federal Assembly, and a majority of portfolios in the Cabinet. Rimmon as the Kirk's financial supremo, and Gilchrist as its spiritual head, moved their households to two mansions on the shores of the Firth of Forth, where they set about living in splendour − on the rare occasions they were there.

In so small a country as modern Scotland − a mere 3 million inhabitants − it had been amazingly easy to conduct this Revolution. Yet, thought Rimmon to himself, it is not over yet. We are not yet a true Church, for we have not yet martyred our own God.

12
Jelly Roll Blues

*By night on my bed I sought him
whom my soul loveth: I sought
him, but I found him not.*

———— SONG OF SOLOMON 3:1 ————

Edinburgh, Friday 8 August 2042

Four years passed. It was like the slow receding of an ice age, the dwindling of the snow, the thawing of glaciers into motion. For forty years men had locked their energies away inside themselves, like animals hibernating in their burrows. But now the winter of despair had silently departed. Folk realised they were no longer afraid of God, no longer afraid of themselves, for they knew that nothing could disturb the benevolence of time. And whether it was God or evil they no longer feared, and whether these two things were or were not the same, they felt released, uplifted, invigorated, ready for the first time in a generation to stare each other in the face without the protection of a plastic visor. They could even look squarely again at the big blue eye of heaven. People whispered of a new Enlightenment, of a new Elizabethan age, and soon there was a plethora of little companies, setting plans on foot for the resettlement of England, for the exploration of France and Germany, for the rediscovery of North America, passing by way of Iceland like Erik the Red. The Earth lay empty before them, theirs for the taking. And the horizons of Scotland no longer defined the limits of the world.

Four years passed not only in the universe men happened to experience, but equally in all the other ones that co-existed with it. In each of these, an infinitely bifurcating Gilchrist, an infinitely ramifying Jenny, an endlessly self-sundering Alec Jamieson had gone their separate and mysterious ways. They split whenever they made a decision, one choosing black, his twin white.

106

They split whenever the world made a decision for them.

In one of these multiple worlds radsuits no longer existed. There came an August afternoon when Alec, now 33 and depute headmaster at John Gregson Academy, found himself shopping on Princes Street. One of his other selves had been delayed no doubt by a mote in his eye, so that he had missed the electrobus. Another had missed the bus anyway, because its driver had been in a hurry for the depot, where a charming semi-mutant conductress awaited him. A third . . .

However, in Herenow on Friday 8 August at 1.43 and 20 seconds, there went Alec, running up the steps to the first storey of Carnegie's Department Emporium. And there, descending in the opposite direction (for she too had not been delayed by a breakdown in her chauffeur-driven carriage, nor by hesitating too long over her purchase of underclothes on the second floor, nor by . . .) came Mrs Jennifer Gilchrist, her extravagant and expensive curves moving as smoothly as ever, her lips as they always had been, parted slightly in astonishment, but a misty expression in her eyes which Alec did not remember.

Both of them stopped, Alec half past her, half swung towards her. She too had turned towards him, her lips open even more rosily.

'Jenny! I mean Mrs Gilchrist.'

'Alec! It must be six years . . .'

They hesitated, then held their hands out, he using the pre-Salvationist 'hello', she the formula of her Kirk — 'May your world be mine.' The mist in her eyes was like a veil worn to conceal pain.

It was only then that Alec noticed the figure of Virgil Appelbaum hovering in the background, along with a couple of very plain mutant maids. Virgil advanced, giggling more confidently than he used to do, but still giggling, and as Alec shook his hand he thought to himself — People don't change; they just wear their gaucheness with more aplomb as they get older.

Behind him a Morningside lady said in disapproving tones: 'Would you maind not blocking the steairs?'

The five figures on the steps parted. In Ifwhere they no doubt split up in a different fashion, but in Herenow Jenny and Alec found themselves squashed together as the Morningside lady inclined her head with a regal 'Thaink you', meanwhile fraying her way upwards and onwards with a furled umbrella, and as her two friends followed her with a 'Thet's so keaind' and a 'Veery obleaiged to you, Ai'm shure.' As for Virgil and the mutant girls, they were pressed together on the opposite side of the stairs.

Alec and Jenny, gazing perforce into each other's eyes, were saying:

'Fancy meeting you like this.'

'It's nice to see you again.'

A pause.

'I don't see why we shouldn't have "coffee". I'm only shopping.'

Jenny beckoned to her maids, herself now somewhat regal. Which was not surprising seeing the expensive clothes she wore, the air of wealth that surrounded her. 'You carry on. You have the list. Virgil knows just what to do. I'll meet you at the carriage.' She consulted her watch. 'Three o'clock?'

They shook hands and parted according to the formula of the Kirk:

'Pick the right path!'

'Don't miss the way!'

By 'coffee' was meant herbal tea. Alec, conscious of the worn patches at the elbows of his jacket, led the way to the top storey of the shop, where a corner window terminating at knee height gave a view across Princes Street Gardens and onto the grandiose bulk of the Castle perched on its volcanic crag. It was a day of haar again, so that the Castle seemed a flat silhouette, its turrets and slanting roofs mere outlines against a white, half-luminous mist.

'Trolls' breath from Norway,' said Alec, grimacing at the weather.

'Aye,' she said, 'nobody lives in Norway except for trolls.'

'Well . . .' They were silent, looking at each other.

'You look even prettier.' It was true perhaps, but Alec thought that the lines of smiling he remembered around her mouth had been replaced by creases of self-pity. At the corners of her eyes, by the tear-ducts, the flesh was slightly discoloured.

'What are you doing now?'

Alec told her of his career. Somehow he had never got round to taking up his ambition — to be a settler in one of the new English communities. He had resigned from the Auld Kirk School after Jenny's dismissal, and gone to John Gregson's.

'And are you married? Surely some nice young lass . . .' Jenny's eyes flicked to his left hand and away. There was no ring, the customary sign of fatherhood.

Alec shook his head and used one of the accepted euphemisms: 'I've often cast the dice, but never thrown a three.' For none of his girls had ever become pregnant.

'Och, I am sorry. The Kirk helps a bit, of course. Are you a member?'

'I'm not a Salvationist,' said Alec, 'and I've never found that it gives any comfort at all. And you? Two children, the papers say.'

Jenny replied, with some of her old briskness: 'That's right, and both of them normal, thank God. Isla, she's nearly four now — a real little madam, you should see her dressing up like an Angel!'

'Like an angel?'

'Like one of the Choir, I mean, all frou-frous and long lace mittens to the elbow. A real bundle of trouble, but she does make me laugh. And wee Peter, of course, his second birthday'll be next week. Very advanced for his age. Do you know, he started talking at 8 months, very young for a boy. Going to have the gift of the gab like his father.' Alec couldn't tell if this remark was approving or the opposite.

Jenny added, 'I can't say the weans or I want for anything . . .'

The intonation was wrong, thought Alec. Her sentence sounded unfinished. 'But?' he prompted her.

A sigh was audible from the other side of the table. She turned her eyes away and gazed at the haar-grey silhouette of the Kirks Assembly. After a pause she said, again with affected briskness, 'Well, it's perfectly natural with Peter so busy all the time, such an important man now.'

'Practically a god,' said Alec.

'Och, he wouldn't like to hear you say that.' She began to laugh, one hand up to her mouth as if to keep the sound in. Alec thought it sounded just slightly unnatural. She cut off her laughter like someone turning a switch. 'Never mind, the weans are a joy, and it's good to be kept busy. You wouldn't imagine how much there is to do, though we have a nursemaid and ...'

She turned towards him again, and it was as if it hurt her slightly to look at him. Alec knew exactly what the matter was, for what was the gossip of the town? 'You have a large household, I suppose.'

'Aye, bigger than I like to think, for it's the old mansion of the Marquis of Queensferry and two whole wings of it are Peter's offices, full of secretaries and ...'

And, thought Alec, if the gossip pages tell the truth, several ex-members of the Choir of Angels, each with her bairn upon her knee.

'But life isn't just a bowl of roses, even in Peter's world, and what cannot be mended must be tholed.'

Alec felt angry hearing the tone of self-satisfied misery in which she said this. 'That's not like you, Jenny. You'll be talking next of duty and crosses to bear, just like old Mairi McInnes.'

'You know, Alec, I've often looked back to old Mairi McInnes as you call her, and thought she was right about a lot of things.'

'*Never*,' he began. But she had abruptly got up and was saying to him in a strange voice — 'Alec, do you mind if we change seats?'

'Of course not,' he said, surprised. As she sat down again, he realised she had wanted to turn her back to the room, for she was fumbling in her handbag, blindly struggling to pull out her handkerchief. 'I'm just like the haar,' she said, trying to laugh at herself, 'all mist and wetness.'

Concerned, he said, 'Don't greet, love.'

'I'm sorry, I'll be all right in a minute.'

The confession began.

'It's terrible, Alec, you can't imagine how terrible it is. Peter has such a magnetism about him. When I first met him I thought it was his melancholy, his air of tragedy — that's why I fell for him, and he *was* unhappy, terribly unhappy at the time. It was irresistible. His fertility, too, it's an awful thing to say — no, why should it be so awful? — these days, when there's only one chance in six of having a bairn, even if you spend life changing religions and wearing your knees out every knight praying in a

110

different kirk! And then he needed to be looked after, he was such a lost little boy and to begin with — och, I was a fool — that's all I thought I was doing — being motherly. Have you any conception, Alec, what a maternal instinct is like in twenty-first century Scotland, when there are so few weans? Why, it's like sex if you're a man — if you're a man like Peter,' she said bitterly.

'And then, you see,' she went on, the handkerchief clenched wetly in her fist, the tears beginning to dry on her face, 'there are books from the twentieth century that tell you all about converting people. I've often wondered if . . . if Peter had read it before he . . . if that is why . . . But that's unfair,' she muttered to herself. 'After all, it's *true*, what he preaches, isn't it?'

She turned her eyes onto him for support, then remembered that he wasn't a believer. 'It's very hard for prophets, the temptations are much stronger, much more frequent.'

Alec looked at her narrowly, but there was no trace of irony on her face.

A delicate female cough sounded behind Jenny's right shoulder, 'Do you wish another pot of coffee?' It was the waitress, hovering inquisitively.

'Megadeath!' cried Jenny. 'I said I would meet them at three sharp!'

'Well — Science take it! — they'll have to wait. I can't traipse through the public streets all teary and smeary. The Saviour's own wedded wife. What would the journalists say?'

Alec nodded to the waitress.

'Converting people?' he prompted.

'Aye, well, Peter has this . . . charisma. But it's not that, it seems, so much as the fact that he converts people. The preaching breaks down their resistance, they become suggestible. Once they've started taking their oversuits off, it's hard to stop.' She began to laugh again. 'The Marquis of Queensferry's house is like a harem, full of young bitches on heat.

'And do you know what he said to me?' she cried, flicking back her hair, then having to flick it back again. 'Do you know what he said? He had the face to say this to me.

' "In Ifwhere," he said, "it'll be a different story. In Ifwhere there are other doubtcomes. I'll be faithful to you there." '

111

She gazed out across the gardens at the inscrutable silhouette of the Castle eight hundred yards away. The waitress set down another pot of tea beside them.

13

High Society

*There were two men in one city;
the one rich, and the other poor.*

—— II SAMUEL 12:1 ——

Thursday, 30 April 2043

In Edinburgh, spring is a sceptical and cautious season. The trees do not blossom in that ecstatic manner of the south, the green of their leaves quite submerged behind a profusion of pink and white blooms, but put out their blossom more cannily, more sparingly, knowing it will soon be vandalised by the cold North Sea winds. So green dilutes the pink and white, and spring is hardly noticed, even as you walk through the chilly breeze and trample its petals on the street.

The most spring-like sight in Edinburgh was Jenny, herself all pink and white like a luscious southern season, snaking her naked self off the bed and into a skirt and jumper. Alec lay back, hands behind his head and admired her, still slim and supple despite the two weans she had had. How intensely satisfied he felt in his body and his emotions! And that intensity was rendered more acute by the knowledge that, soon, she would be away to Queensferry once more – that their relationship was not only incomplete but permanently threatened.

'Jenny!' he said, sitting forward and gazing at the threshing jumper inside which her head was hidden. 'Come away with me!'

The jumper stopped writhing about and for a moment was perfectly still. Then Jenny shrugged her shoulders energetically and her face emerged. Putting her hands to the nape of her neck, she eased up the strands of hair still caught inside the collar and shook her head to make them fall free. She gazed at him, her lips slightly parted.

113

'Come away with you!' she repeated in amazement. 'Where ever to?'

'One of the colonies – Andy Clelland's offered me a place – the new Ripon community. It's going to be set up at the start of June, and they need teachers.'

'Teachers? Do you mean me?' She added doubtfully, 'Isn't it *radiant* down there?'

'Och, they tell me the level's no worse these days than anywhere else. Jenny, why don't you come? What does Gilchrist care about you? A new start.'

' "A new heaven and a new earth",' she said drily. Alec noted she was rather red in the face. 'Alec, do be sensible, do you really want to hide away in the back of beyond?'

'I can remember,' said Alec, 'a lass of 21 who said to me what a pity it was for us all to be stuck fast in Scotland like frightened bairns.'

'And who . . .? Oh!' said Jenny, suddenly remembering that it had been herself, on George IV Bridge, eight years ago.

'Come on, I'll make you some tea, and we can talk about it. There's still time before you have to be away.'

Ten minutes later, Jenny was pouting at her teacup and saying, 'You don't realise how jealous Peter will be.'

'Jealous?' said Alec, astonished at this gambit.

'He would be furious. He has such a temper, he's so possessive.'

'Aye, he likes possessing Mona, Iona, Shona, Fiona . . .'

Jenny winced and said, 'Yes, but you have to understand it's different in his case. He's not like other men, he's . . .

'Not like . . .!' said Alec, becoming moment by moment more amazed.

'I suppose it's because he's such a creative person, he has all that energy to spare. You can't expect a man like him . . .'

Alec struggled to suppress his feelings of anger, and said, 'Look, why are we talking about *him*, why don't we talk about ourselves? Of course, I realise I can't offer you what *he* can. Compared with him, I'm a down-and-out. No nursemaids, no butlers, no fashionable clothes, no carriages . . .'

'Now *you're* being jealous, Alec,' she said, and since his mentioning it had less to do with jealousy than with finding out

114

how much she cared for such things, a reluctant suspicion emerged into his mind. Was money really an obstacle?

He cursed himself for a fool. Of course it was. In the practical world it was, and Jenny, once captivated by Gilchrist's failure, had now been ensnared by his success, and it had quite likely spoiled her for any poorer man.

'After all,' she went on, 'what have you got to be jealous of? It's you I love, not him' — snake-like again, she entwined herself gently about him — 'and that's got nothing to do with irrelevant things like stocks and shares. Only you must see things in a practical light. Running away to hide in a radiant desert doesn't solve anything. Anyway, what more do you want? What we have is a real atom-smasher. When we reach fusion, it's melt-down every time. Intercontinental! Do you think it would be half so active in Timbuctoo?'

What more do you want means *what more can I have*, he thought. Particularly if, maybe, two of the things she enjoyed about this love affair were secrecy — and revenge upon her husband.

'Ripon,' he said.

'Ripon's the same thing, isn't it? You mustn't be so demanding. Besides, how could I leave Isla and wee Peter? My husband would never let them go — the children of the Prophet, imagine!'

She had played her trump card, and a good one it was too.

'But Alec, you worry me. Please tell me you're not thinking of taking off to the wilds of Yorkshire all by yourself. You're not going to leave me, are you?'

A little mystified at being so outmanoeuvred, Alec let her climb into her radsuit — so sensible a garment for the illicit affair — sensible too for the local weather, for outside the chill spring afternoon had turned to rain.

'Sure you can't stay for a while longer?' he said, offering an olive branch. 'It's damp and dreich out there.'

'I've got to be back by seven.'

'Och well.' He imitated the gestures of a minister giving a blessing, and intoned, 'Dressed in your radsuit you may not receive the holy suntan of the Kirk.'

'That's better, darling,' she said, and kissed him back, grateful for the lightening in tension.

He thought to himself, he should be grateful for what he'd got.

Jenny made her way out into the pouring rain and stepped into the cab she had called. Fifteen minutes later it deposited her at the mews behind her townhouse, and she let herself in by the servants' door. The coachman would call for her at six, to return her to Queensferry in time for dinner.

The rain fell and fell, sounding like distant applause.

14

Blood on the Moon

*For the good that I would, I do not;
but the evil which I would not, that
I do.*

——————— ROMANS 7:19 ———————

Friday 15 May 2043

On 15 May, at ten past five in the evening, Alec was poring over some sixth form history essays on 'The Theocratic Federal Constitution of 2009'.

'History is fundamentally unpredictable,' he read. 'As the Very Reverend Gilchrist has shown, anything can happen to anyone and, in Ifwhere, it does. History is therefore out of date, for the whole caboodle depends on nothing more than chance. If you're in Herenow it falls out one way, if you're in another world, another way. Why bother with history, then, and indeed, in this essay I shall not bother with it, but will write of how it might have been . . . and therefore undoubtedly was.'

Alec looked up for a moment, sighing. As he did so, the doorbell rang, imperiously, twice.

Hoping that he knew who this might be, he put down his red pen, and gave himself a passing glance in the mirror as he made his way to the front door. The figure on the landing was wearing an oversuit, as he had expected, but the greeting died on his lips as he noticed that the suit was of the wrong colour and that the person concealed within it was unexpectedly broad and tall. Radsuits were now the favoured dress of the Moral Majority. The only others who affected such a garb were those who had good reason for disguising themselves, such as adulterous wives and husbands, burglars, and the like. Alec at once assumed that this must be a book-burning evangelist, and he was about to close the door again when the figure removed its helmet.

There was Gilchrist gazing in at him like a bugaboo out of a nightmare.

Then Alec did slam the door shut, but hesitated as he heard the letter-box open and Gilchrist's voice coming through it, uttering the Christian greeting 'May your world be mine!'

'Are you alone?' said Alec after a moment's uncertainty.

'Are *you*?' replied Gilchrist, laughing.

Alec felt a twinge of the angry guilt that sometimes afflicts a man who is sleeping with another's wife. The anger outweighed the guilt, for *he* had nothing to be ashamed of. But it was reasonable to feel just a wee bit alarmed at this unheralded visit. Might Gilchrist have brought others with him? Some of those expressionless and muscular young men, for instance, that you saw standing at the foot of the platform at his meetings, singing all the hymns mechanically and never allowing their eyes to stray from the crowd. This thought too set the adrenalin going.

'What do you want?' he said through the door.

'Och, just a wee chat, Jamieson. I'm a man of God, remember. I wish you no harm.'

Alec hesitated. 'Just a moment, then, while I turn off the kettle.' Instead of doing this — for the kettle was not on — he went to the window and peered up and down East Claremont Street. No one to be seen, not even a carriage. Had Gilchrist come on foot, then? He returned to the door and reluctantly opened it. The Supreme Moderator stepped through it, offering his hand. Alec took it. ' "Coffee"?' he said.

When the herbal tea was ready, he returned to the sitting room where Gilchrist was standing, inspecting Alec's books. His air of contempt hid a sense of discomfort, however. 'Still teaching history, I see.'

'Aye, and a fine mess you people have made of it. None of the students thinks it matters any more. They think they can do what they like with the past, and with the future too.'

'You're not saved, then,' said Gilchrist, pronouncing these words in exactly the tone that one would say, 'You've not bought a new settee.'

'I don't need to be saved,' said Alec. 'I'm still a member of the Auld Kirk.'

'I'm sorry about that, *genuinely* sorry,' said Gilchrist.

There was an uncomfortable silence. They sipped their herbal tea and did not meet each other's eyes.

'Aye,' said Gilchrist suddenly. 'Jenny said you weren't saved yet.'

Alec replied, his voice sharp with irritation, 'You haven't come to convert me like one of those travelling god-grocers?'

'No, no, of course not. A man's conscience is his own affair.'

'The way your tabernacles snoop on their converts, nobody would think so.'

There was another silence, and Gilchrist said. 'It's amazing how difficult this is.'

Alec said, 'I'd hardly have thought you of all people would be at a loss for words.'

'There's no need to take that tone,' said Gilchrist. 'Look here, this is all too *lento e pianissimo*, as Virgil would say. Would you care for a proper drink?' He delved into the capacious pockets of his radsuit and produced from them a full bottle of whisky, which he set on the table between them. Then, as a second thought, he took off his oversuit. 'It's the very best, of course. I brought it to show there were no hard feelings.'

'No hard feelings about what?' said Alec, though he did not doubt that the subject of Gilchrist's interest must be Jenny. He produced glasses and poured both of them a brimming tumbler. 'Good health, It's over six years since we set eyes on each other, if I remember rightly.'

'God's health.' said Gilchrist. Since the carriage had missed him in Heriot Row, seven years before, he had not allowed a drop of alcohol to pass his lips. Why should he need it, he who knew the truth? Besides, it interfered with his control over people. Here this evening, though, it seemed necessary again. It was the only way to get his tongue to say the words he had decided on. 'Aye, over six years. I've often thought, Jamieson, what a pity it is that we lost contact.'

I haven't, thought Alec, but he said nothing and waited for his unwelcome guest to make the first step. Gilchrist, however, was

119

thinking to himself that false positions were fine when it was others who were in them. It would be easier in a minute when he had had another wee dram. He had forgotten how comforting whisky was. In the meantime, let them put up a pretence of friendly reminiscence.

'Do you remember that night in the Mortar and Pestle?'

'The non-singing folksinger . . .'

'Aye, it's a well-kent sort.'

'Two hours, and he sang three songs.'

'And *they* were rubbish.'

'Have another dram.'

'Aye, I will that.'

'It was jokes all the way and chords strummed between them. And every now and then you'd think he was going to sing, but he never did.'

'Thank Christ.'

'I remember he told the one about . . . What do Winnie the Pooh and Attila the Hun have in common?'

'I don't remember, what *do* they have in common?'

'They both have the same middle name.'

'And when the bell rings for time, he cries out, "There's a leper come in!" '

'Jenny couldn't thole it.'

'Have another dram.'

'Aye, I will. Will you not have one yourself?'

'Aye, I will. *Slainte.*'

'*Slainte.*'

They fell silent, their reminiscences being depressing, and not helping to make them feel warmer towards each other.

'A nice flat you have here,' said Gilchrist without conviction.

What's the good of that, with no woman in it? thought Alec. Aloud, he said 'Not bad.' Unwillingly he added, 'I suppose the fireplace is eighteenth century.'

'Nineteenth,' said Gilchrist.

'Handsome, though, isn't it? Adamesque and . . . handsome and . . . makes you feel it's a long time before Quantum Physics.'

Gilchrist winced.

'Your glass needs filled.'

120

'So it does. Aye,' said Gilchrist again, but with an equal lack of conviction, 'I regret losing touch with you.'

Why does the man have to repeat himself, and what in Science is he here for? wondered Alec, worried because he thought he knew only too well. His unease at being the third corner in this ill-assorted triangle, his dislike of the man — and a distinct undertone of fear, for Gilchrist, however dislikeable, was now practically above the law — spilled over into annoyance at this piece of hypocrisy. 'Nonsense, Gilchrist, we never liked each other, you know that as well as I do.'

Deep inside himself, Gilchrist had no confidence in his likeability. Consciously, he prided himself upon it, confusing it with the way he could sway a thousand souls, the way he could make lassies fall at his feet — both in and out of crowds.

'Nonsense, Jamieson, we were always the best of friends.'

Alec took another draught of whisky and said, 'And Jenny? Were we friends over her?'

'Now look here, Jamieson, you know very well it was she that set her cap at me, and not the other way around.'

Alec was aware that this was the case, but the fairness of the comment made him angrier.

'She had only one idea in her head, Alison, from the day she set eyes on me,' continued Gilchrist, shaking his head to indicate how little responsibility he had in the matter.

'Who?' said Alec, thinking he had misheard. 'Who had?'

'Jenny,' said Gilchrist, looking at him in equal surprise.

The fact that he, Alec, an insignificant and ill-paid dominie, was a person who could be trampled underfoot at a flick of Gilchrist's finger, the fact that (despite his anger at Gilchrist's behaviour to Jenny) his own conscience was not entirely clear, the knowledge that this man whom he had jealously disliked from the beginning was now one of the two or three richest and most powerful men in Scotland — and, more shamefully, the fact that Gilchrist was indecently fertile whereas he, to his best belief, was not — all this, not unaided by several glasses of best Islay malt conspiring against an empty stomach, converged to make him lose his temper.

'Your own wife! You can't even remember her name!'

Gilchrist looked at him in bewilderment, for he was unaware that he had just called Jenny 'Alison'. And indeed this was hardly surprising, for in his dealings with the Choir of Angels, and with other prospective members of it, it was the easiest thing in the world to call Maggie 'Mairi' or Fiona 'Shona' or Shona 'Sheila'. In Ifwhere they might have been so called, and doubtless were. The dance of the atoms. The dice of destiny. The thousand paths. In the perspective of eternity, in the vast and benevolent view of God, such things had little significance.

Alec, meanwhile, continued his outburst, recounting Gilchrist's behaviour as it had been described to him by Jenny, charging him with perfidy, cruelty and indifference.

Perhaps it was not so much Gilchrist's cruelty and indifference to Jenny in the present, but rather Jenny's cruelty and indifference to himself in the past — and his fears of it in the future — that so distressed him. But Gilchrist, remembering (as he often did these days) that the second half of his name was a guarantee of rectitude, began to protest. He had, he reminded himself, come here to this grubby little flat in one of the just slightly less desirable quarters of the city; he had gone through all the pain of steeling himself to do so, and with the best intentions; he had come here in a spirit of generosity and self-denial. Not that it was particularly generous to give away something that you no longer wanted. But he had put off all sorts of important appointments that concerned the welfare of Scotland to talk to this shabby little teacher. And he was rejected! Besides, he *did* feel guilty about Jenny. He had behaved despicably towards her. The more that Alec told him that, the more he could not bear himself, and the more he felt like taking Alec by the throat.

The still, small voice of Gilchrist's doctrine now spoke to him out of the clamour of his emotions. 'And why not?' 'But,' said his conscience, 'I have not the right.' 'But,' said his doctrine, 'the paths always branch. You cannot hurt him, for in Ifwhere things will fall out differently.' 'But . . .' 'Nonsense, the paths are many, it is only out of Herenow that he . . .'

Whatever it was that had prevented Gilchrist from striking his accuser was silent for a moment, and the Supreme Moderator of

122

the Kirk of Instant Salvation aimed a fierce blow at Alec's mouth.

Alec fell back, feeling at his jaw. His hand came away with blood on it and at the sight all self-control deserted him. There was a pause, then a noise of buffets, punches, gasps and curses. There was the crash of a chair overturned, and a further crashing and thumping as two heavy male bodies fell to the floor, pummelling blindly at each other. A shrill jagged noise as the whisky bottle, two-thirds empty, was swept into the hearth, where it smashed. Another chair went over, and the little table was crushed to smithereens. At last, Gilchrist, heavier than Alec and taller by four inches, had his hands round his throat and was choking the life out of him. ('Why not?' said the still, small voice. 'If anything can go right, it will. So nothing can go wrong.') In the silence there was the sound of someone in the flat below, banging on the ceiling with a broomstick.

'Mr Jamieson? Mr Jamieson?' cried little old Mrs Munro from underneath the floor. 'This is a quiet neighbourhood!'

Gilchrist's right hand suddenly felt as if it were made, not of flesh and blood, but of torn muslin. He noticed that there was blood all over the floor. Somehow, he must have cut himself in the fight. He released Alec, who crawled away, clutching his throat, eyeing his assailant with fear.

'Sodomy and incest!' swore Gilchrist softly.

Silence. Even the broomstick downstairs had stopped striking against the ceiling.

Gilchrist spoke in a very quiet voice, grasping his wrist from which blood was pouring.

'I think I've done something to my hand. It must be the whisky bottle. Would you mind feeling in the top flap of my jacket and calling the number you find there? It's my personal physician.

'No, no, not the hospital.

'And — I'm sorry — but would you mind hiding my radsuit? It would be gey awkward for the Supreme Moderator to be found with one of those.

'This is daft,' he said after a pause. 'I came here to . . .' He was very white in the face. 'I came here to say you could have Jenny.'

'Very generous of you,' said Alec bitterly, having returned from the phone.

'She had no idea I was coming here, of course.'

'Of *course*?' said Alec incredulously. 'You treat her like a redirected mailbag.' He felt gingerly at his bruised throat. It hurt him to breathe. 'And what about the children?' he asked.

'The weans?' said Gilchrist, and fainted clean away.

Alec set about staunching the flow of blood from the Moderator's wrist.

15
Baby Won't You Please Come Home?

*He shall return no more to his
house, neither shall his place
know him any more.*

JOB 7:10

Saturday 16 May 2043

Alec had a broken tooth, a split lip and a discoloured right eye. He tucked a scarf into his shirt to conceal the worst of the bruising round his neck, but he did not, he decided, look a pretty sight. He paced the sitting room, restlessly awaiting Jenny. What had she heard from Gilchrist by this time? He had tried to telephone her last night, the moment Dr Ferguson and his private ambulance had left. But Mrs Gilchrist, he was informed by the indifferent voice of the maid at the other end of the line, was out.

Not that it mattered. She was seeing him tomorrow anyway, and it might be better to tell her about it face to face.

Though somehow he knew that it wasn't. He felt distinctly uneasy waiting for her. She was three-quarters of an hour late already, and a strange certainty was growing inside him that she was not going to come after all. He gazed out into the street through the cracked window-pane. It must have happened in the fight with Gilchrist, but he had not noticed it till this morning. Where in Einstein's name was she?

Just then the doorbell rang. No it wasn't, he realised with a sinking heart. It was the phone.

'Alec?'

'Yes. Jenny darling!'

'Listen, Alec, I . . . Peter's hurt himself, did you know that? God knows how it happened, he won't tell me.'

'I know he has. Where are you phoning from? Come straight on down here, darling, and I'll tell you all about it.'

'I can't do that now, Alec,' she said rather shrilly. 'I was phoning to say I wouldn't be coming today.'

'Why, what's happened? Tomorrow, then. I must see you and tell you . . .'

'No, not tomorrow, Alec. Things have changed, you see, and when I saw Peter come home like that, I just knew . . .I can't . . . I know we've been very happy these last few months, but I can't leave him *now*.'

'Jenny,' said Alec, 'I love you and I want you and the truth about last night is that your precious husband attacked me and nearly murdered me and . . .'

A burring sound down the line made it clear that she had already put down the phone.

Calls to her Edinburgh town house had no result. When he rang Queensferry, the same impassive maid informed him that, 'Mrs Gilchrist is not at home to callers.'

So it was that Jenny broke off her affair with Alec without telling him that she was pregnant — by him and not by Gilchrist.

Wednesday 20 May 2043

It was several days before Rimmon (on urgent ecclesiastical business in New Rome, now once more named Glasgow) could be called back to the capital. When at last he arrived, on the fifth day after Gilchrist's accident, he noticed that Jenny had banished all the Angels to Edinburgh and taken charge. She spoke to him in private first.

'Peter,' she said, 'is very low. He almost reminds me of how he was when we first knew him. Poor lamb,' she added, dabbing at her eyes.

'The last thing your Peter is, is a poor lamb,' said Rimmon. 'A shepherd, yes, and on occasions a lost sheep, but not a lamb.'

'Och, Archie, do take me seriously for once. You know what I mean.'

'I know exactly what you mean, Jenny. Describe his state of

126

mind to me, and then I shall go up and see for myself.' To himself he thought, she's found her baby again.

'Well, he's very depressed, Archie, and do you know? — he's talking of retiring from the leadership of the Kirk and going off to bury himself in some — on some — in some castle on some island somewhere, and Archie, you *must* talk to him. Nothing *I* say makes any difference!'

'Ah!' said Rimmon, 'How very interesting.'

Meanwhile, the Supreme Moderator sat in an armchair in his bedroom waited on hand and foot by his wife, and brooding to himself in a state of gloom and self-doubt such as he had not experienced since the days after Alison's death, seven years ago. Even the cheerfully frantic tones of 'I've found a New Baby' (Bechet and Johnny Windhurst, April 1945) were insufficient to lift his mood. Sidney's music was sheer incandescence, but he was viewing it now as if from a distance, imprisoned under a roof of Highland raincloud, watching other rainclouds scurrying in from the Atlantic. In a moment the rift of moving sunlight would disappear, the horizon would vanish, he would find himself in a narrow glen, whose exit was veiled by rain, where the very atmosphere was weeping.

Moreover, listening to Bechet — a thing he had not done now for years — made him uncomfortable. Here was the free, the spontaneous, the improvised, yet, even prestissimo, every note was struck with perfect timing and attack. Where did the old Creole catch his breath? How unlike those inferior musicians who pour forth an urgent flurry of notes, all slurred, in a hasty fumble of keys! Bechet's music had become, he realised, not merely less than a consolation; it was positively painful to him, because it formed such a contrast with the music of his own Kirk, as if it were trying to make him aware of a cheapness in its message. Or rather, not in its message, but in the methods he had so consciously used in putting it over. He pressed the remote control button and switched the music off in the middle of a soaring updraught of joy — then cursed himself, for it was like shooting an eagle in mid-flight. Now the sunlight had really gone out, and it was he who had extinguished it.

How shaken he had been to discover that his religion — his

127

own personal revelation — had made it easier for him to kill someone. For, let us not pretend, that was what he had been about that night, like some drunken mariner in a brawl, trying to throttle his wife's lover. But worse than that was the fact of the still, small voice, whispering in his ear, 'Go on, do it, what does it matter, it's only in Herenow!' He thought of the court case he had seen reported in the *Herald* that morning, and frowned.

Not that he could ever lose his faith. Too much hung by his keeping it. How could someone who saw his own certainties reflected nightly in the eyes of a thousand mesmerised converts ever doubt himself? Ah now, that was a good question.

The indignity of it! That the Choir of Angels — or indeed that pasty-faced lass from Ullapool — were gossiped about in the press had never bothered him. In Ifwhere you were often married to someone else. The only difference was that (as the popular joke ran) he had some of his Ifwheres in Herenow. No, it was the ignominy of being involved in a ... in a *fait divers*, a vulgar brawl. Perhaps he would not have minded so much if the hurt had been only to his spirit. But to wound himself so stupidly!

He gazed through the window and out over the gardens, framed in evergreens, themselves framed in turn by the Forth's blue waters, beyond which the hills of Fife lay in a fitful succession of sunlight and shadow. But the sunlight was darkened by his own gloom, and the view, beautiful though it was, had an air of unspringlike chill.

He had mismanaged the interview with Alec — mismanaged it disastrously. He should have put himself in charge from the outset, told the man just what was going to happen and how. Instead of which, he, the preacher, the manipulator of crowds, had allowed a private interview to arouse first diffident and then violent aspects of his character — aspects which he had thought suppressed for ever.

He must cling to his faith.

But his faith was precisely the thing that, at that last critical moment, had betrayed him.

The seven-foot door into Gilchrist's bedroom came slowly ajar, then, after a moment, opened expansively. Rimmon strode in, with his secretary in tow, and said in the appropriate tones:

128

'Gilchrist, how are you feeling? I was appalled to hear . . . No serious damage done, I hope? The hand . . . Are you too tired to . . .?'

Between these expressions of concern, Gilchrist made reassuring noises. No, it appeared that no tendons or nerves had been severed. Yes, he felt fine, considering. No, it was a more personal matter he wished to discuss.

As he said these words he was aware that his arm was hurting him. The fact did nothing to reconcile him to himself.

'We'll not be needing Catriona, then.' said Rimmon, and dismissed the secretary with a nod.

'Did you see the report in today's *Herald Angel*?' asked Gilchrist.

Rimmon gazed at him with interest, taking in the flat intonation, the general air of despondency. He was reminded of the Gilchrist he had met sitting over a whisky in Deacon Brodie's tavern eight years ago. He turned his attention to the newspaper report.

'Jeremiah Forbes, 29, chain-store manager, accused of the murder of his wife Kathleen, openly admitted today at Glasgow High Court that he had strangled her. He pleaded not guilty on the grounds that . . .'

Rimmon, his narrow mouth expressionless, glanced up at the headline under which this little item lay. 'CHURCH DOCTRINE PROVES HIS INNOCENCE, DEFENDANT CLAIMS.' Without blinking, Rimmon continued to read.

' . . . on the grounds that his Church, the Kirk of Instant Salvation, exculpates him from blame. He reminded the Court that, according to the Kirk, *all* the decisions that a man might take are in fact taken by him, in each of the various worlds through which his consciousness passes. If not in Herenow, then certainly in Ifwhere. He went on:

' "So you see that in *one* of the possible universes, I was *forced* to commit this crime. But if I was forced to commit it, I cannot be held responsible."

'This statement by the accused caused uproar in court, which had to be cleared.

'The jury retired and are still considering their verdict.'

'Well?' said Gilchrist, who had been following Rimmon's reactions closely. Nothing showed in his associate's face as he handed the paper back.

'A clever man,' was all he said. To himself he thought, Gilchrist is a genius of a kind, but he does not look far enough ahead. I always knew there was instability there. Could this be the moment? He was silent, waiting for Gilchrist's commentary.

The latter sighed and changed the subject. He began to talk about his feelings. He was tired, he said, and the burden of six years' continual preaching was beginning to tell. He needed a rest, or something longer than a rest. As he continued to speak, the aching of his arm became confused with his state of mind. If he could clear his conscience, resign his responsibilities, he felt, the pain would cease.

'You perturb me,' said Rimmon, injecting some concern into his tone. 'Are you seriously considering giving up your position at the head of the Kirk, and with it your evangelical work? Can that really be your meaning? I must be misunderstanding you, forgive me.'

Gilchrist shook his head and repeated that that was exactly what he meant.

'You must see,' said Rimmon, 'that I cannot take such a suggestion seriously. Why, what would become of the Kirk you have so brilliantly founded? Its fate rests in the hands of a single man, yourself.'

'Och, I cannot believe that,' said Gilchrist. 'Plenty of fine preachers have emerged over these last few years. Campbell, Bateson, Lauder, MacFadden. I should be leaving the Kirk in good hands.'

'Not in such good ones as it is at present. You must excuse my asking so personal a question, but, Moderator, *what is the state of your faith?*'

'As strong as ever,' said Gilchrist irritably.

'Well then, this must be just a passing mood. Naturally you feel depressed at being confined to the house in this way. The accident has probably been more of a shock to your system than Dr Ferguson recognises. Forgive me for pressing the question, but let me put it this way. You recall that appalling moment —

130

how could any of us forget it? — when you were approached by a young man on the stage at the Kelvin Hall — a young man with a gun. You behaved, I recall, with true spiritual self-possession. Buoyed up by your unshakeable faith, you told him that the gun would fail to go off — in Herenow. And, of course, so it did.'

Gilchrist nodded. 'My beliefs are quite unchanged. Were another Moralist to step in here the next moment and point another gun at me, I should be just as confident. Indeed, I should welcome it as a test of truth.'

'I rejoice to hear it,' said Rimmon, in a tone that almost approached the pious. 'You mean that, visualising yourself at the mercy of that armed fanatic, you . . .' And Rimmon painted as vivid a picture of the attempt on Gilchrist's life as he could, watching the Moderator's face closely as he did so. What he saw seemed to satisfy him, and he leaned back in his chair, repeating the words, 'I rejoice to hear it.'

'But it makes no difference,' said Gilchrist with a grimace. '(Science blast this arm of mine!) My mind is made up. I want to withdraw out of the limelight.'

Rimmon wondered to himself how Gilchrist's hand could still be paining him after five days of the most modern medical care. It must be his mind that hurt him. Aloud, he said, 'Well, there would be no harm in a holiday, even a longish holiday. I have just the place for that. You will recall that the Kirk has recently bought Kildonnan Castle as a retreat and conference centre.'

'Aye, on the Isle of Eigg, isn't it?' Rimmon always knew 'just the place', as he had back in 2036.

'That's the one. One of those fine old Scottish baronial mansions, with its tower-house built after Glamis, its guest wing after Drumlanrig and its drawbridge after Cawdor. There you will have all you could wish for — isolation, tranquillity, comfort, sea and mountain, exquisite scenery. Your whole household could move there for a month or two — even longer, if you wished. You would need some of the Choir of Angels to provide spiritual and musical consolation.'

Gilchrist, stung, looked up, but no trace of sarcasm showed in Rimmon's face.

The Kirk's financial manager now painted as vivid a picture of

Gilchrist's contentment on the Isle of Eigg as he had just done of the attempt on his life. On his lips it sounded, except for the serpent and a shortage of Mesopotamian sunshine, exactly like the Garden of Eden. 'Of course, the Castle is not *quite* ready. I am hopeful that in three weeks at most . . .

'However,' he concluded, 'I am sure these feelings of yours will pass. A temporary depression, very natural in the circumstances.'

Rimmon kept closely in contact with his superior over the next few days and, on the following Wednesday, felt that the time was ripe for his next move. Gilchrist in the interim had hardly stirred from his first-floor bedroom and was still to be found there staring gloomily out over the waters of the Forth which, truth to tell, could not be seen at all today, a grey fog having drifted in from the North Sea as if called up by the Moderator's suicidal mood. An exceedingly pretty housemaid was fussing round Gilchrist, and Rimmon, knowing his man, was intrigued to see that he showed no interest in her.

After a few preliminaries — Christian greetings, inquiries after Gilchrist's health and morale, a brief account of the Kirk's latest dealings on the Stock Exchange — Rimmon got down to business. Preparing the way with mentions of the Moderator's unshakeable faith and of the ravishing attractions of the Hebrides, watching his victim with intense care all the while, he finally arrived at the target he had been seeking all this week.

'Well, if your resolution is so firm, Supreme Moderator, I shall not stand in your way. I can only say that the Kirk will be cast into desolation by your retirement. Your presence is irreplaceable, and it may be that everything we have worked for these last six years will be brought to naught. However — I hesitate to put these proposals to you, but I have been thinking them over with the greatest care this past week, and I feel my duty compels me to bring them to your notice. Stop me if at any moment you feel the slightest qualm.'

The calm formality of Rimmon's speech gave an appearance of sanity to the astonishing proposal he now unfolded.

'Gilchrist, old friend, there is a way — and, I believe, a foolproof way — of ensuring that your retiral from the active life of the Kirk

132

will not have the disastrous effect it might otherwise produce, but on the contrary bring us converts in possibly greater numbers even than before. Shall I explain?

'I shall have everything prepared at Kildonnan Castle for your arrival there, and perhaps you would like to think over which Angels you would like to attend you, and whether your wife should know of all this or not. Give me a list of all the items you wish to have shipped out there, and I will have the whole thing organised with the utmost despatch.

'Having prepared your retreat, we shall then be able to proceed to the next part of my plan — if, that is, you are willing to assent to it.

'Here is what I propose. And indeed, I am tempted to think that no more spectacular departure could ever have been contemplated. We shall model ourselves, dear friend and associate, upon the failed attempt by that foolish young assassin five years ago. You will be preaching, a shot will ring out from the front of the congregation, you will — apparently — fall dead. Naturally, this piece of vaudeville must take place in front of the largest possible audience, so as to have the greatest possible effect ... You will be universally mourned, your death will be praised as a martyrdom, as the supreme witness of a great spiritual leader to his faith, and converts will flock to the Kirk. It will deal the *coup de grâce* to other sects.

'Meanwhile, of course, you will not be dead at all. You will have been spirited away to the halls of Kildonnan Castle, where, across the Sound of Arisaig and far outside the reach of prying journalists, you will be able to find release in that life of quiet contemplation you so yearn for.'

Rimmon fell prudently silent as a maid entered the room bearing a bottle of Glenlivet for himself and a glass of herbal tea for Gilchrist.

When she had left he went on, 'It goes without saying that if a single word of this got out, the whole project would be spoilt.'

Gilchrist was silent, gazing at Rimmon, and the latter wondered — though without any feeling of concern — what he might be thinking.

'I do not know whether my proposal seems to you a mite

unconventional. Let me take the bull by the horns. For example, the word "deception" might have crossed your mind. Dear co-religionist, we have been through so much together. Together we have suffered, prayed and borne witness to the truth. Together we have saved a million souls and swept away the old despairing Scotland. You will recall that long ago we discovered that God's truth on the one hand, and its mode of presentation on the other, are two quite different things — as far apart as the meaning of a word and whether it is spoken, written in ink, stuck upon a billboard or chanted by an angel choir. We decided long ago that the means we use are immaterial, for *it is only the truth that counts.*'

There was a long pause. Slowly Gilchrist inclined his head, in the slowest and most thoughtful nod that Rimmon had ever witnessed. Most thoughtful and therefore most deliberate.

He passed briskly on.

'One of the advantages of this plan is that you would become "King over the water". For my part I firmly believe that, after some little time spent upon Eigg in contemplation of the Lord's mysterious purposes, you will come to see your retirement as a mistake. Dear old friend! You will come to regret your decision, and long to return to the world of men — and women — and to the excitements of evangelism.

'Now it is obvious — is it not? — that there will be no difficulty about this. No difficulty at all. With your charisma and my talent for publicity, with our joint skill in mounting the enthusiastic meeting, the spectacular crusade, there can be no problem. Another three years, my dear old friend, and *we shall stage your resurrection.*'

There was a long silence, as Gilchrist studied first Rimmon's narrow lips and then his own hands. No, he hadn't lost his faith. He had no doubt about the Branching Paths. The problem was that their truth made all choices equally good, and by the same token all choices equally bad. He had removed evil from the world, certainly, but it had been replaced, he now saw, with a yawning void of pointlessness which his energy, his enthusiasm in preaching the Message had hitherto disguised from him. The thought gave him satisfaction, for it reflected his mood. He had remade the world in the image of his own despair.

134

16

After You've Gone

*Precious in the sight of the
Lord is the death of his
saints.*

──────── PSALMS 116:15 ────────

Edinburgh, Saturday 6 June 2043

'Have you tried Virgil?' asked Helen after a pause.

Alec thought she was prettier than she had been when he had last seen her — seven years ago, was it? Small, plump and blonde, her eyes and mouth big and round in a round face, she had had the charming chubbiness known as 'puppy-fat' — a sort of mistiness about the contours like the haze about a harvest moon — not quite finished, not quite firmed up. Now she *was* firmed up, in spirit too, though there had always been a hardness inside that delectable softness. Alec realised that what he had taken for 'gold-digging' — her throwing herself at the prosperous Rimmon — had been just that, but not in the way he had thought it. As a younger man, he had imagined that young women simply 'fell' for richer, older men, as ripe fruit fall from a tree. In Helen's case this had not been so. There was a cool mind hidden inside that exaggeratedly doll-like face. She had always known she was a match for Rimmon.

This cool mind would not, and probably could not, help him now.

'He's in charge of the household at Queensferry, as you know,' Helen went on. 'He did try to get married on several occasions, always to the same Angel. But he kept having unlucky accidents. The first time he broke his leg the day before the wedding. The second time he broke an arm, though why that should prevent a

135

wedding I can't imagine. The third time — and then the poor lassie went and died. In Herenow, that is. It's really very sad.'

Alec felt sceptical about her saying it was very sad, then realised that she meant it. His respect for her increased.

'Aye, I've tried Virgil,' he said. 'He was at his most irritating. He shimmered, you know what I mean? He gobbled and dithered. He told me he couldn't imagine how he would set about saying such a thing to Jenny.'

Helen nodded.

' "Should I do it *appassionato e molto con brio*?" he asked me. "Or *lento e dolce*?" I told him it was for him to decide, because I didn't know how he stood with Jenny. So he said he'd try, but I could tell from his tone of voice that he wouldn't.'

'I know exactly what you mean.'

They were sitting in the Rimmons' enormous drawing room, one lofty storey above ground level, gazing south towards the ruins of the Science Faculty and the treeless Pentland Hills. The Rimmons had taken this big town house in the Grange district a couple of years before, leaving the two older sons the residence in Heriot Row. The garden behind the house was an acre of flowers and sloping lawns, but from this height Alec could only glimpse the tips of the trees as a gust of North Sea wind held them in its spasmodic grip. The day was bright and blue, for the wind was too fierce for clouds; and Alec thought to himself that it had something of the sunlit coolness of Helen's own mind. The weather too confirmed that reason was not with him.

Helen poured him more tea out of an antique teapot brought back from England (decontaminated, of course) and sat down nearer him to explain.

'You need a friend, a close friend, but do you and Jenny have friends in common any more? I will do what I can, but I'm bound to tell you . . . there's something you obviously don't know.

'Jenny's pregnant.'

Alec sat stock-still, the teacup halfway to his lips. 'Whose is it?' he said, setting it down untasted.

'I don't know.' She fell silent, not looking at him.

'But you suppose,' said Alec bitterly, 'judging by her behaviour, that it must be Gilchrist's.'

136

'Don't you?'

Alec was silent, looking much cast down.

Helen said, 'I promise I will do what I can. But do you really suppose that all your Ifwheres are full of no one but Jenny? I think you should put her out of your mind, if only because she's grown accustomed, *a*, to having an immense amount of money and, *b*, to being a martyr. It's terribly nice being a martyr, you feel so virtuous, like a little ray of sunlight in a darkened world.'

Into the middle of Helen's irony and Alec's gloom — sunlight lying slantwise on the wallpaper, the wind in the garden blowing the heat out of the summer — walked Rimmon himself, showing no surprise but plainly wondering who this shabbily dressed stranger might be. Helen rose composedly and introduced him.

'Alec Jamieson? Seven years? Jenny's old school? Forgive me, I don't remember. Och, a history teacher, are you?' All this was said in a tone of indifference.

The indifference, however, must have been less than total, for having poured both of them a drink, he settled down to questioning Alec on the size of the school he taught in, the proportion of Salvationists to be found among its pupils ('40 per cent, excellent!') and the reactions they had to lessons on the Holocaust. Had their views of it been changed in any way by the Salvationist movement? Did they view it with less horror than children brought up in other sects? Meanwhile, Helen had gone out for more tea, and Alec felt somehow paralysed. The armchair he sat in had removed all the strength from his limbs and he knew that, much as he disliked Rimmon, the man had him in his power until — abruptly no doubt — he would choose to throw him out.

'As a historian, now ...'

Alec protested. He was a mere teacher, a server-up of other people's theories and facts.

'You are too modest,' said Rimmon, in a tone that suggested that he was *not* too modest. 'No, no, as a professional historian, I should like to ask your opinion of the psychology of religion. What is it that makes people "believe", as they put it?'

The inverted commas round the word 'believe' made Alec wonder how Rimmon himself would have put it. Doubtfully, he said, 'Belief is natural to human beings, I suppose.' He paused, feeling how banal this statement was. It was uncomfortable to be pulled away from his personal preoccupations with Jenny.

'That's not what I meant,' said Rimmon impatiently. 'I wondered what it is that makes some beliefs much stronger, much more convincing than others.'

'Well, I can see that Salvationism is highly attractive,' said Alec cautiously. 'It offers so much hope — a near certainty of happiness both in this world and the next . . .'

'Ah, but that's not what makes people believe in it,' said Rimmon, and proceeded, under the pretence of asking Alec his opinion, to offer his own.

'I do not know, Jamieson, if you have studied the human soul as dispassionately as I have. Perhaps it has to do with my inside knowledge of the Kirk of Sigmund Freud.'

'And Von Däniken.'

'Are you *sure* you're Alec Jamieson?' wondered Rimmon. 'Strange how I don't remember you.

'No matter. You remember that to Freud, the unconscious no longer sees opposites as contradictory. Let me give you the obvious example.

'It is always said that persecution spread and popularised that tiny eccentric sect called Christianity. If it had not been proscribed it would not have become the religion of the Roman Empire. Now, how is one to explain that? Do folk in some way *welcome* martyrdom?

'The Communist Kirk of the twentieth century is even more interesting. A Russian Communist had the immense advantage over a Christian of being both martyr and persecutor at one and the same time! His religion was able to appeal to both types of psyche, the sadistic and the masochistic.'

Alec protested. 'But I thought it was its idealism that made it so popular — its promises of welfare and social justice.'

'I am afraid the facts support no such interpretation. The Communist Kirk certainly *promised* health, happiness and equality. But it achieved them so much less than the nations of the Capitalist faith, while at the same time engaging in such blatant militarism, exploitation and savagery, that it is unthinkable anyone was really taken in. It must therefore be the exploitation and savagery that were the secret of its appeal. After all, do you recall the figures? Sixty million Russians, killed by their own regime over a period of forty years!'

'Well yes,' said Alec, 'that is Kurganov's estimate. But what makes you talk of Communists being both martyr and persecutor at the same time?'

'You recall how the old Bolsheviks "went to the stake" under Stalin? They stood in front of the firing squad and professed their loyalty. Extraordinary, isn't it?'

'So what is your explanation?'

'It is very simple. Humane and gentle creeds carry no conviction. They have no intensity. A faith begins to look real only when people begin to kill or die in its name.' Rimmon pointed outside the window at the evening's windy glitter. 'Sparks of sunlight, as the trees toss — is that a fact? No it is simply the play of light upon the leaves. A mere surface. Maya, the Hindus called it.

'The worship of Kali, on the other hand . . . You recall how her devotees used to go out into the dark byways at night and strangle innocent passers-by. There's something real for you! The goddess Kali, an immense hypnotic fact, daubed red and black with darkness and oblivion.

'And that is why all churches need martyrs and why so many of them have been persecutors too. Christ and Torquemada are but two aspects of the same creature. To the human being, Jamieson, nothing is real unless it hurts.'

Helen, serving fresh tea, smiled gently and said, 'You are a cynic, Archie.'

'Cynicism is a form of optimism,' replied Rimmon sententiously, ' — a method of not suffering from one's pessimism.'

The moment Alec's cup and glass had both been emptied, Rimmon rose to his feet and explained that he had work to do. 'It is good to see old friends again, but you would not credit the amount of things I have to take care of. People envy me, I am told. Well, they should just try to take on my job. So grateful to you for listening to my amateur views on your subject.'

'I'll see you out,' said Helen.

Alec felt depressed after his conversation with Rimmon, more so (he felt) than the content of it warranted. He believed Helen when she assured him on the doorstep that she would do what she could, and brushed his cheek with her lips. But he knew now that it would all come to nothing.

17
When the Saints
Go Marching In

Sunday 26 July 2043

'Is that you, Andy? — Aye, I've been thinking it over and the
answer is yes. Do you have room for a history teacher? — Och
well, I can remember my two times table. — Yes, yes, B U I K,
book, will that do for you? — When do we start? — No, man, I'm
not impatient, I just want to get the hell out of Scotland. — Nature
study, well, I could always say how the birds rarely bee these
days. — Gee-whizz, a kibbutz? Where there's wife there's hope.
— Durham? Aye, I ken fine where it is, but are the natives friendly?
— Assegais and pitchforks, grand, but what's the local religion?
To tell the truth, Andy, I'd rather they didn't have one. —
Wednesday 20 August. I'll be ready waiting. — Yes, just myself. —
No, Andy, I'll be waiting, I'm sorry to have havered for so long.'
  Alec put the phone down.

A glittering web had been suspended in the air, as from a multitude of human spiders, spinning electric cables between tree and
tree, from which hundreds of bulbs dangled — a net of lights
intervening between the lawns and flower-beds of the Gardens,
the black bulk of the Castle rock, and the endless reaches of dark

sky above its turrets. Under the trees, crowding the steep grassy slopes, packing even Princes Street beyond, all that could be seen was thousands of faces, white as death in the artificial light, and the glint of eyes all turned expectantly towards the empty stage. There, in a few minutes, the Service of Affirmation would begin, and the Prophet (healed at last from his long illness) would speak again to his faithful. They had come from as far away as Galloway, Morar, Skye, Buchan, John o'Groats and even across the Pentland Firth. Despite the crowd's immense size, it was cheerful and good humoured, as for a military tattoo or a fireworks display.

Backstage behind the empty bandstand (the centre of all this expectation) Gilchrist was standing, revolving like a slow teetotum, his hand being shaken at every point of the compass by helpers, minions and friends. 'It's been a gey long time ... ten weeks without the Lord's anointed ... no manna in the wilderness ... now the Lord's message is in safe hands again ...' Gilchrist nodded and smiled, half deprecatingly, wondering who was sincere, who envious. Returning to the point where he had started, he put his arm around the shoulders of Alasdair MacFadden, and drew him aside to settle a few last details. Rimmon appeared from the far edge of the stage and banished the helpers to their various posts, and suddenly the wings were empty, save for Gilchrist, Jenny, and Virgil, hovering uneasily in the background. 'It's just like the old days,' said Jenny, 'so exciting! Hotching with people. Like Perth in 2037.' Her lips were parted rosily on the delights of memory.

'Aha,' agreed Gilchrist who, for his part, was wishing the whole harlequinade was already over.

'How many people are there out there — fifty, a hundred thousand?'

Twenty feet away, Virgil's lips were moving, perhaps in time to the word *moderato*. His arms wagging, he took a step forward towards them, then paused abruptly, like a phantom uncertain whether it should emerge from Ifwhere. What a tonic to one's faith Virgil was!

Jenny said, 'The crowd's all singing, singing like ...' She winced, because she'd been about to say 'like angels'.

Gilchrist felt touched. He would not, he recognised, have felt

142

anything like so touched if he had told Jenny the truth. As it was, he felt sorry for her, and hoped she would not spend too long dressed in widow's weeds, but soon — well, why not? — make contact again with her wee school teacher.

But now he had other things to preoccupy him. The whole vast throng of spectators had fallen silent as the first candles of the procession were glimpsed winding their way down the Mound. Virgil had vanished as if whisked away upon a spell. Taking Jenny by the arm, Gilchrist kissed her tenderly but with little regret, and shooed her off towards the reserved seat that awaited her among the expectant worshippers.

He was alone. All was ready for the last sermon.

In Rimmon's old house on Heriot Row, the present occupants, his sons aged 25 and 26, were playing Dungeons and Dragons. Apart from the fast carriages they drove, the hang-gliding in summer, the horses they owned and the ski-ing they did at Aviemore, they had no other interests in life. They spent money but showed no desire to make it. Their eyes never followed a shapely pair of legs down the street. Rimmon attributed it to the fall-out, and placed all his hopes in Helen's children, who were still too small to disappoint them.

Ian the elder son was playing a nine-foot pirate called Captain Kidd, Stewart the younger a three-handed dwarf named Bolg. Kidd had infravision and a magic cutlass. Bolg was clairvoyant and could fight off six Orcs simultaneously with his eyes shut. They had just entered a noisome cavern through which luminous green water was flowing, whistling gently to itself as it went. 'Will you listen to the tune?' asked the book of instructions. 'If so, turn to no. 157. Will you close your ears and run out of the cavern? If so, turn to no. 89. Will you slash at the water with your sword? If so, turn to no. 341.'

Ian, or rather Captain Kidd, turned to Stewart, or rather Bolg, and said, 'You have precognition, so you're allowed to peep at the next numbers.'

'If you slash at the water, it snaps at your sword and swallows it whole,' said Bolg, consulting the book. 'If you turn and run, the roof falls on you. If you listen to it, it's singing *I Know that You*

143

Know and then . . . I'm only allowed to look one step ahead, but och, it'll be nothing but a Siren. Or maybe a Medusa.'

'Let's stand and fight her,' said Captain Kidd, putting plugs in his ears, a shade over his eyes, and mentally whetting his cutlass.

Inside the little cubicle where Gilchrist was standing it was as black as the Lord High Inquisitor's heart. He viewed the lighted scene before him through a slit, not unlike the visor in the old over-suit he had worn for so long. Before him he could see a segment of the crowd stretching up towards the railings of Princes Street, or rather he could see the tops of a thousand heads, for these were all humbly bowed in his direction, as MacFadden, in his ringing and melodious bass, led the prayers. A complete cross-section of heads, shiny white bald ones belonging to old men, lumpish and earless ones belonging to mutants, the long curling ringlets (whether red, blonde or dark) that were the modern sign of a woman of proven fertility. To the left of this oblong picture (which Gilchrist supposed must be rather like looking at a tele-vision screen in the old days) his vision was partially blocked by the huge Tree of Many Branches that was the emblem most used by the Kirk. As a tree, it was, of course, also the Cross. But it was a strange tree, having all its branches upturned and pointing towards heaven in representation of the diverging paths of human fate. Thus some of the branches terminated in black hoods like the headgear of penitents, these specks of darkness barely visible among the multicoloured blaze of candles that crowned most branch-tips, symbolising the lighted paths of consciousness and (ultimately) the hope of resurrection. In fact, it looked very like an inverted Christmas tree.

He thought to himself, I have changed the world.

But was it truly he that had changed the world? If his doctrine were the truth — and despite his feeling of depression and pointlessness he still believed it was — then this labyrinth of paths that he had trodden since the evening of revelation in Heriot Row had been chosen for him and not by him. Herenow, in which he stood behind the backcloth, ready to advance into the brightness of the stage and the hush of human adoration, was but one of the worlds that might have emerged from the seed of that

144

moment ... and all those that might have emerged inevitably must. It was like that game that Rimmon's half-witted sons spent their time playing, with its scenarios full of alternative possibilities. All the words foretold, all the worlds foredestined by Shiva, the six-armed God.

If, then, in a moment, he stepped out into the 'theatre' of the Gardens, to speak to his faithful and be, like an actor, apparently shot down, would that be his decision, or would he be merely play-acting? Would he be play-acting at play-acting? To expose himself to a sham assassin's imitation bullets — would that count as a decision? And what, in his view of things, was a decision? Merely the point at which his consciousness would divide and pursue two independent courses of action. By disposing of evil, it seemed, he had disposed of choice.

He could always leave by the back, slip away into the anonymity of the darkness beneath the Castle's huge volcanic shadow. Or could he? Leaving by the back of the bandstand, he would also be leaving himself behind — that other self who would *not* leave, but who would step out onto the stage to confront his non-assassin.

Could he tell by the way it *felt* whether his decision was real or not?

'White Blood!' said Captain Kidd. 'You were nearly turned to stone there!'

'Just as well I can fight with my eyes closed,' said Bolg. 'It's a cleverer stunt than Perseus's. Even so, I was lucky I threw a thirty-three. Do you think this adventure is becoming a little too much for us?'

'No point in going back now,' said Kidd. 'You must pick up skill and intelligence points for that. Aha, very satisfactory.'

'Medusa's head too,' said Bolg. 'Give me your magic cutlass.'

The room they were playing in, with its velvet curtains, its comfortable leather armchairs, its shaded golden light falling upon the polished walnut table, faded from their awareness. They stood knee-deep in water, in an evil-smelling tunnel deep underground. An eerie green light shone out of the water illuminating slimy walls of scarred and uneven rock. In the stream at their feet lay the corpse of a beautiful woman half submerged. It was head down in the water, and some of the snakes which it wore instead of hair hissed and flickered their tongues with a last dying impulse, as if lifted on a sudden current in the burn.

'Ugh!' said Bolg with a shudder, realising suddenly that he was frightened. He took the pirate's weapon carelessly in his third hand, cutting his finger. It stung like venom, and he cursed, nearly dropping it in the water.

He hacked at the back of Medusa's neck, feeling faintly sick. It took several blows of the magic steel to detach the head. While Captain Kidd looked steadfastly in the other direction, Bolg hauled it up by the hair, having time once again to notice through his shut eyes the unearthly, heart-stopping beauty of the face before he stowed it in his knapsack for safe keeping.

'That should come in handy for the next monster we meet,' he commented. 'Where now?'

Ahead the stream emerged from an archway in the tunnel. The two adventurers stepped through it, Bolg with his eyes still closed, but seeing through the shut lids, Captain Kidd, his cutlass back in his hand again, glancing nervously about him. In front of them, though muffled by the walls of rock, a distant screaming could be heard, as if from a woman in fury or torment.

It speedily became clear that they were in an underground maze.

The passage swung left, then right, then left again. It parted into three ways, then two, then four. Before long they were thoroughly lost.

Midnight. Gilchrist stepped out onto the stage, holding his arms aloft to receive the plaudits of the worshippers. They for their part did not cheer or clap, for this was a pure and sacramental moment, but merely sighed with one accord, involuntarily, so that a great breath went sweeping out across the crowd, the length and breadth of the Gardens to east and west, stirring the air, making the leaves upon the trees quiver; and the sound came soughing back into Gilchrist's ears like the swish of a quiet wave lapping on a shingle beach.

146

Deeply moved, Gilchrist began to speak, softly at first, almost whispering his words into the microphone, while behind him, fixed to the backcloth of the platform on which he stood, those other symbols of the Kirk looked down on him impassively – illuminated stained glass likenesses of Bohr, Einstein, Schrödinger, Wigner, – an image of Christ breaking the bread and fishes, and another of a shower of particles colliding and parting in a cloud-chamber.

While he spoke it was as if he had two selves, one speaking, the other thinking its own independent thoughts. He was for some reason vividly aware of the mixture of light and darkness in the air in front of him, how the arc lights marked out a boundary in space, making the atmosphere almost visible, so that light itself seemed turned into a palpable mist, whereas beyond these areas of illumination there lay a transparent emptiness, where darkness was absolute. It was somehow the opposite effect of his experience on Arthur's Seat eight years before, for here tonight the lighted space in which he spoke seemed like a flimsy veil floating upon a deeper, more fundamental darkness.

Why have I let myself get into this predicament? he asked himself. It is clear that, accepting the doctrine of my Kirk, the assassin's gun will, in at least one possible world, contain real bullets, that in another he will not be here at all, that in a third some eager worshipper will overpower him before he can fire, that ... It did not matter, nothing mattered, because whatever happened, he, Gilchrist, would survive in some of the possible worlds. At all events he was determined he would not be persuaded back into preaching, he would retire to Kildonnan Castle, never to return. For, if Ifwhere was real, the very fact of having preached its reality was merely an accident of fate. He had thought to give the world a meaning, at long last, after uncountable centuries of suffering and fear, a consoling, compassionate meaning. He found, instead, all meaning had been withdrawn from the world, and replaced by the indifferent dance of atoms.

But if, whatever happened, he was determined to retire to his Atlantic island, was that not a decision? He faltered for a moment in his address, then picked up the thread again.

147

'Last Judgement!' whispered Kidd, his teeth chattering, as he gazed into the darkness at the centre of the maze.

They were both exhausted after a long hour's trip through the underground labyrinth, and had several times resolved to turn back. But it seemed that, however they twisted and turned and vainly sought to retrace their footsteps, this was no ordinary labyrinth, but rather sucked them in steadily towards its centre, as if by some attractive force. Perhaps the planet we dwell on is alive and, entering these rocky caverns, they had by some terrible mischance been caught in the digestive tract of the Earth itself.

It was a few moments before they could even see what was confronting them, and then it was only because the creature hidden in the darkness before them uttered a sound. It screamed again, ear-splittingly, as if it were suffering the most excruciating pain, and the sound issuing from its open jaws created somehow a light which faded as the sound faded, but in which for a moment the monster itself could be seen.

It was human in shape, but scrawny and skeletal, coal-black, and wearing only a tiger skin around its stick-like thighs. It wore a necklace made of human skulls, its withered breasts hung down to its knees, and it had not two arms but four, in which it held a sword, a bow, a noose and some other instrument whose purpose they could not guess. The most horrible thing of all was its face, for its teeth were like rotting fangs, it had three staring bloodshot eyes (the third being in the centre of its forehead) and its hair stood on end like a bugaboo. Perhaps indeed it was as frightened as it was frightening, and all the more dangerous for that.

Kidd now understood why he had been unable to see the thing, even using the infra-red wavelength, for it was the same death-like temperature as the cavern walls about them. As for Bolg, he was fumbling desperately with his knapsack. At last he got it open and, clenching his teeth in revulsion, grasped hold of the snakes, now clammy and lifeless, which crowned Medusa's head. He held it up, in the gesture of Perseus rescuing Andromeda.

In the blackness ahead of them, the creature laughed, and as it laughed it could be seen once more, rising to its feet and taking a bird-like step towards them. 'Fools,' it sniggered, 'that is myself.'

148

One of the worshippers in the front row, a little dark mutant just below Gilchrist, was leaning forward in eager attention, feeling in his breast pocket as if for some devotional tract. A gun appeared in his hand and, without warning, he was firing it straight at the Moderator. All the way up the slope to the broad street behind, the Gardens were filled with screaming. Some at the back stood up, craning their necks to see what was going on below. Down by the stage, people fought each other to get away from the squat little man, still seated, firing his gun. Folding chairs were tipped up, women stumbled over them and were trampled on by those behind.

At the first shot, Gilchrist sat down on the stage in amazement, feeling at his chest. He opened his mouth, and attempted to croak out the words 'You can't . . .' but no sound came. His legs would not hold him, so he began crawling forward to the edge of the platform, still soundlessly mouthing, trying to explain to the assassin that he couldn't possibly kill him, that it was quite pointless to try. He had totally forgotten that this was supposed to be a pantomime, a piece of theatrical deception. Reaching the front of the stage, he received a bullet full in the forehead and had the sensation of falling endlessly inward, inward into himself, as if he were a neutron star clenching upon itself, pulling its own light into its core, crushing itself out of existence. His last sensation was one of astonishment.

The assassin too looked astounded by what he had done. He seemed mesmerised by Gilchrist's body, lying with one arm over the edge of the stage like a deflated dummy – and his eyes were still fixed upon it as he docilely allowed himself to be disarmed. Shaking his head, he was led away.

Bolg and Captain Kidd sat looking at each other, in the pool of lamplight cast on the walnut table.

'Throwing dice against the goddess Kali,' said Bolg at last, shaking his head in disgust.

The adventure was over, for they were both of them dead.

18

Slipping and
Sliding

*Think not that I am come to send peace
on earth: I came not to send peace,
but a sword.*

——— MATTHEW 11:34 ———

Sunday 3 February 2048

'What time's the appointment? 9 a.m. tomorrow?'

'That's right. Archie, I hope you don't mind, but I've changed to Doctor Mears. You see, I was worried. Our old doctor's a Salvationist, and I wondered if he really *cares*.'

'Do what you think for the best, dear.'

'Oh Archie, I'm scared. Our little girl . . . I do hope she can stay in Herenow, with us.'

Not since the frosts of 1981 had there been such a winter. In November the temperature sank day after day, till it stuck at minus 20 for a three-week spell, and the barmen in the pubs joked that their beer was a bargain, for it was twice as dense as it should be. The pavements were ice, polished and polished again by passing footsteps, the air was sharp in the nostrils, and Arthur's Seat crouched on guard above the city, lion-like as ever, but wearing a thick polar coat of white. Even in full sunlight, the air had a purple haze, as if the crystals suspended within it were not of ice but of amethyst. In early January the snows returned and the temperature dropped again to much the same point. Duddingston Loch under the mountain was frozen over from the boathouse and the crags at one side to the reedbeds at its further shore. The geese, bewildered, went slithering across the ice, seeking for a patch of water.

For three weeks the wind was mesmerised into stillness. Then

150

it suddenly felt colder as the temperature rose, the humidity increased, and the wind resumed its old habits. Mrs Jenny Gilchrist, whisking through the Queen's Park in her heated carriage that Sunday morning, waved like a queen herself to the strollers and wondered, as she passed by Duddingston Loch, if it were really safe for the skaters still to be crowding the ice. Salvationism should make you more aware of the different outcomes or 'doubtcomes', more careful to avoid them, though she was aware that when she had broken off with Alec five years ago, she had been able to console her conscience with the thought that, in Ifwhere, another Jenny and another Alec would have − 'osmosed', as the modern jargon went.

The carriage turned into the drive of the minister's house, overlooking the loch and Prestonfield House beyond it, and drew to a halt. The horses stamped and blew, their nostrils making dragon's breath in the chilly air, and Mrs Inglis the minister's wife came running down the path − 'So *delightful* you could come, so *sweet* of you to agree' − already in full gush before she had even opened the carriage door.

'Such a *kind* thing to do, so busy and *important* a person as yourself, and to take time off − from your children too − so as to talk to all my Sunday school pupils and give them the news of God's Infinite Mercy.' Never had capitals and italics been so audible, thought Jenny, as she replied that it was nothing, in such a good cause. However, she knew that it *was* good of her, she *was* very busy, opening bazaars, shaking hands, making little speeches here and there, keeping the memory of the Founder and Martyr alive. This was a much more demanding task she was facing today − a class full of adolescents, just like that unforgettable (and unforgettably troublesome) group back in the Auld Kirk School all those years before. How they had opened her eyes! she thought, what a debt she owed them! Children of that age had such lively minds, such a free spirit of inquiry.

Now the inverted commas sounded in Mrs Inglis's voice as she cooed, 'But you must have a strengthening cup of "coffee" first, Mrs Gilchrist, before we "throw you to the lions". You'll have met my husband, of course, but he'll be so pleased to have a word with you before the "fun" starts.'

151

The Reverend Inglis came out on the steps beaming, perhaps a little nervous. He was a tall clarinet-shaped man with a voice to match. Indeed, it reminded Jenny of those old soprano sax records that Peter had been so fond of.

'My father's staying with us too,' confided Mrs Inglis in a whisper, 'but he's out on a walk, thank the Lord. I'm sorry to say you'll be meeting him at lunch. Though one really shouldn't say such things about one's own "flesh and blood", I'm bound to say he's a terrible old curmudgeon — such an *irreligious* man. Whatever would have become of my Soul if I hadn't met my dear Husband here, I simply Shudder to think!' She gazed fondly at the minister's long equine nose and squeezed his arm.

Perhaps it's their age that makes them look so sullen, thought Jenny, half an hour later, as she gazed out from her pulpit over the rows of adolescent faces and listened to the minister introducing her — 'Such a great honour for our little congregation' — or perhaps it's the fact that Sunday morning catechism is going to be much longer this morning. To tell the truth she was sorry for them, just as she had been for that other class of hers thirteen years ago. She supposed that they looked at her in rather the same light as Corinthia and Susan and that other class had looked at Mrs McInnes the headmistress — come to impose an alien way of thinking, that of another generation, on minds that were interested, at the moment, in only one thing — the alarming and fascinating processes in their own bodies. She would try not to bore them too much.

So it was that she cut her speech a little short and came to question time a wee bit too soon for comfort. If she'd only been longer about it, there wouldn't have been time for that last nasty question. The girl who posed it was plainly going to be a beauty, with her big black eyes, her matt white skin, her glossy hair.

'Mrs Gilchrist . . . Why did William Reoch shoot your husband?'

'Sandra!' exclaimed Mrs Inglis, shocked, then tightened her lips. That girl always had been a trouble-maker and would come to a bad end.

'I don't mind, Mrs Inglis,' said Jenny. It was all a long time ago now, and she could think back to it quite calmly. 'Sandra's your name, is it? Well, we shall never know exactly why, because some

152

indignant members of the Kirk did something very wrong — they broke into the jail and killed him before he could be brought to trial. The only thing we have is a statement he made to the police, in which he claimed that, as a mutant, he would be better off dying, because in Ifwhere he would be a normal.'

'But that's right, isn't it, Mrs Gilchrist?' said Sandra, speaking up as bold as brass. 'His soul would find itself somewhere else at once.'

'It doesn't excuse him killing the Founder, though,' said Mrs Inglis indignantly.

'But the Founder too!' said a lad on the front row, 'he's only dead in Herenow, isn't he? In Ifwhere — in lots of Ifwheres — he's as large as life!'

'But that doesn't make what he did right. Killing is always quite wrong.'

'Even if you can't really kill anyone?' said the boy. 'Why is it wrong if you don't do them any harm after all?'

'Well, that simply shows, eh . . .'

'Kenneth,' Mrs Inglis prompted her.

'It simply shows, Kenneth, that it isn't the harm you do to others that makes it wrong, but the harm it does to yourself.'

'Besides, if you've been properly brought up,' said Mrs Inglis, who found it impossible to keep quiet even when there was an eminent visitor in the church, 'such a thought would *never even occur to you!*

'Yes, Ishbel?'

'Mrs Gilchrist,' said the new questioner, a lass with a halo of bright red hair, 'my little sister Kirsty's caught white blood . . . and the doctor says she's going to die. Mrs Gilchrist, isn't she *real*?'

'I'm sorry, Ishbel, I don't quite understand. What did you say?'

'I asked if she was *real*, Mrs Gilchrist.'

'Of course she's real, dear.'

'But I thought the Kirk said that people who are in pain aren't real, their true selves are really in Ifwhere where they're happy. Is Kirsty just a *shadow*?'

'I don't think you've got that quite right, Ishbel. You see, a person remains a person till the very *last* chance is gone. I expect the doctors are doing all they can, and in some of the worlds of

153

Ifwhere, one of their cures is *bound* to work. You really don't need to feel afraid for Kirsty. That's just how I felt about my husband.'

'Ought I to feel sorry for Kirsty, then?' asked Ishbel, staring at Jenny out of unsmiling blue eyes.

'Of course you should, dear,' said Jenny. 'Our feeling sorry proves that God must be good, because it shows us how unthinkable it would be if He weren't.' She stopped suddenly in her explanation, for she could see at once that she had lost them. They were all gazing at her in incomprehension, with the exception of little Sandra, who said,

'So if we stop being sorry, it stops being unthinkable?'

Jenny opened her mouth to reply, but the lassie went on, 'What if there *isn't* a chance?'

'How do you mean, Sandra?'

'I mean what if someone's in terrible pain and it's bound to go on for a long time and they're sure to die? Are *they* real?'

'What a morbid subject,' said Mrs Inglis. 'You really shouldn't be thinking about such things at your age, Sandra.'

Jenny broke in: 'It's all right, Mrs Inglis, I'll answer the question. To be honest, there must be some cases like that, but not very often, because almost always there's a chance. Now such a person would be a ... a shadow, as you put it. But you see, we can't ever know in advance, can we, who was a shadow and who wasn't?'

Sandra opened her mouth to say more. But Mrs Inglis thought this discussion had gone on quite long enough. She rose to her feet and gave a short speech of thanks to 'our eminent visitor, the Mother of Holy Kirk', followed by a quick hymn. The children filed out, their eyes already brighter, whispering and giggling.

It was strange, thought Jenny, as she followed her hostess and the minister in to lunch at the manse. Was it because these days she was used to speaking in public only to grown-ups? Or was it because they had reminded her forcibly of her own favourite class, all those years ago? She had been rather shaken by the bairns' questions.

An old man with long white hair rose stiffly from the fireside as they entered, smiling at a private joke as he held out his hand to Jenny.

154

'This is my father,' said Mrs Inglis, 'Mr ...'

'Sh, don't tell her my name,' said the old man. 'Let's see if she remembers it.'

'Goodness,' said Jenny, lips parted in astonishment, 'it's ... you're ... you can't be!'

'So you remember me, do you? Ah, but do you remember my name?'

'Mr Za ... Za ... It's unpronounceable. Mr Zaleski.'

'Zen' nodded his Einsteinian cataract of hair. 'Right third time, and aren't you surprised to see me still alive, and all the way from Drumbeg to meet you again. I was sorry to hear about your husband.'

Oh dear, thought Jenny, this is like a blow to the solar plexus. She had often looked back on Drumbeg and the brief time Peter and she had spent there as the one idyll in her life. It floated still in her imagination, preserved under its blue and hazy sunshine, unattainable, frozen for ever in cold crystal. The Isle of the Great Deep, that Celtic paradise on whose shore no seafarer could ever land save once in his life and that only if there were some lapse in the deadliness of fate. A very unSalvationist sentiment, but that was how she felt. For a moment her eyes brimmed with tears.

Zaleski noticed, but his daughter certainly did not. 'Father, you're awful!' she cried, by no means pleased. 'Fancy keeping such a thing to yourself! Fancy not telling us you knew Mrs Gilchrist, of all people!'

'Ah, there's a difference between knowing and having met,' said Zaleski. 'And now you can see why I didn't want to greet her before her performance. The sight of my heretical old face would have put her right off her stroke.'

'He uses such impossible old-fashioned slang,' grumbled Mrs Inglis to Jenny. 'Can *you* understand him?'

Lunch was conducted to the incidental music of Mrs Inglis's voice, singing the praises of the Kirk in general and of their distinguished guest in particular, with occasional fugal touches from the saxophonic vocal chords of the minister. It was like question and response at prayer, only the minister in his own house took rather the part of the congregation than that of the

155

officiant. It was not till an hour later, Mrs Inglis being positively obliged to quit them and make the 'coffee', that Jenny could at last renew her acquaintance with Zaleski.

'I'm afraid my husband was very rude to you at our last meeting.'

'Perhaps,' said 'Zen', 'but I have forgotten that.'

After they had inquired after each other and she had congratulated him on wearing his 76 years so well, she said:

'So you're not saved?'

'What a very personal question! My dear, when you look at me so eloquently out of your pretty blue eyes and ask me am I saved, I earnestly wish I was. But no.'

'I'm sorry. I had hoped that, since you were in at the start of it all . . .'

'Since you have asked me so personal a question, may I do the same? You have not remarried?'

'No, the children . . . my duty to the Kirk . . . Peter's memory.'

'Are you sure it's faithful to his memory to be faithful to his memory?'

Jenny turned hurt eyes on him, and he immediately said, 'I'm sorry, but in Ifwhere you must have married again. Why not in Herenow?'

Jenny thought to herself — There are two different sets of things, the ones you know, and the ones you do. Aloud she said, 'I suppose that in different Ifwheres one gives oneself different rationalisations.'

'That is very frank. I'm an old man, Jenny — you don't mind me calling you Jenny? — so perhaps I may be permitted the impertinence. Have you seen today's *Sabbath Apostle*?'

At a loss to understand this sudden switch of direction, Jenny shook her head.

'Let me show you.'

Newspapers are always full of calamities, and this was no exception. The yearly report of the Ministry for Home Affairs was a catalogue of disasters — sectarian riots in Glasgow and Dundee, a surge in violent crimes, a rise in the rates of infanticide and suicide, a shortage of blood donors, an official investigation into the Charity Commissioners' misuse of their funds. The only rays of hope in an otherwise darkening Scotland were the fertility rate and the membership figures for the Kirk of Instant Salvation which, since Gilchrist's martyrdom, had risen to 60 per cent of the population. Zaleski sat back in his chair, pointing to this figure and then to the suicide rate.

'Cause. And effect.'

'Cause and fall-out? What do you mean?' Jenny looked distraught.

'The nation is demoralised. The responsibility for everything has been removed from men and women and given to God. You can be selfish now with a clear conscience, because He will take care, through the infallible device of Ifwhere, that nothing you do can ever hurt anyone else. Since you claim that no one can ever get hurt, everyone always does. You preach, in effect, that people who suffer and die aren't real. Yet our sense of the reality of others is the root of decency. How can you have a good society without compassion? Do you know, I read in the *Herald Angel* the other day of a little boy who trapped his finger in a carriage door. And do you know what the parents did? They walked away!'

Zaleski had gone pale. After a moment he resumed: 'What a paradox! A religion whose motive was compassion — to prove that suffering was unreal and that God was good. But which has turned into finding a universal excuse for that pain. Do you know what I think, Jenny? I think that if you make God perfect, you turn man into a monster.'

Mrs Inglis had returned, crimson in the face on hearing these last words. She thumped the trayful of coffee-cups onto the table with such indifference that they rattled.

'Father!' she snapped, as if he were thirty years younger than herself instead of thirty years older. 'What blasphemous talk! I'm sure you only say that for the pleasure of shocking us. At least our kirk makes sense. We don't say God's a woman, like the Feminists. We're not like those dreadful Anastasites who claim that Christ is risen and amongst us — now! — incognito! — no one knows where!'

'Perhaps you Strippers make too much sense,' said the old man.

157

'If we thought that every stranger might be Christ, how differently we'd act!'

'But this is awful,' said Jenny in a whisper. 'If you are right, Mr Zaleski, there's a *reason* for there being evil in the world.'

'Exactly,' said Zaleski. 'Or maybe it merely shows that it's not a good idea to think you know all the answers. And even less of a good idea to think someone else does, even if it's Someone, with a capital letter.'

Jenny said, her eyes popping, 'But do you not believe in God?'

'I'm not saying that. God is there, or something very like Him. But He refuses to be defined. He lurks in the uncertainties between all certainties, in the spaces between all solid things.'

'You mustn't mind my father,' said Mrs Inglis loudly to Jenny, though it was obvious from her face that she minded him very much. 'His brain isn't as clear as it used to be.'

It was about three in the afternoon before Jenny left the manse, pensive and somewhat troubled in mind. She mounted into her carriage and Finlayson the coachman drove off. A wholesale thaw had set in, the short steep hill outside the manse was gleaming black and, as they reached the foot of the slope and clattered through the park gates, the horses nearly shied and bolted as they came upon a sinister figure walking towards the village of Duddingston. It was dressed all in white and carried a white stick. As the horses (not being Strippers) fought to avoid running it down, the carriage slewed round in the road, and with a thump came to rest against the railings at the head of the steps leading down to the lochan. Jenny was thrown against the opposite wall of the coach and sprawled there dazed for a moment.

Finlayson, cursing all the geniuses of science, descended to inspect the damage.

At the window, just six inches from Jenny's eyes, there appeared the blind man's face, turned full on, as if he were sighted and looking in at her. But that was impossible, because there were no eyes in his head, nor any place where eyes should be, but simply a flat smooth surface continuing up from his pallid cheeks, so that his head looked like a large white rounded pillar on which some practitioner in black humour had pasted a pair of red lips and a pair of eyebrows.

Jenny screamed and shrank away, but the vision was already gone. Shaking, she fumbled at the door-catch and almost fell out onto the road.

The blind man was already two hundred yards off, tapping his way along the edge of the pavement just beyond the gates of Duddingston Church, pacing along almost as fast as if he had eyes. Nonetheless, it was surprising that he had already walked so far.

Finlayson was still cursing and heaving at the carriage's bent wing, so Jenny turned her attention to the scene around her. She cast a casual eye in the direction of the lochan, wondering if she should return to the manse for more fortifying 'coffee' while the coachman wrestled with his problem. It was only then that she noticed that the skaters had all withdrawn to the edges of the ice, and that they and others on their Sunday outing were standing in a half moon peering out across the frozen loch, all focusing on a single point. Against the wall of the boathouse a couple of ladders were leaning, but no one had gone to fetch them, and the crowd, perhaps some hundred persons in all, were motionless, in silent concentration, as if at some theatrical spectacle. In the centre of the loch, perhaps a hundred yards out from the shore, something black flapped and waved upon the ice. A faint cry came to her ears, and she realised that the moving figure was not upon the ice after all, but floundering in deep water and shouting for help.

Jenny ran down the steps to the lochanside as fast as their icy surface would permit and, approaching the nearest man, said, 'There's a boy in the water. Why doesn't somebody do something?'

Turning, she shouted up to Finlayson, still busy with his carriage.

To the stranger she said, 'Look, there's a couple of ladders by the boathouse wall. It wouldn't be difficult . . .'

Finlayson had straightened up, and was wiping his hands on a cloth with painful slowness. Since the man beside her was gazing at her as if she were mad, Jenny approached someone else.

'There's a wee lad in the water, he'll drown if you aren't quick.'

'He won't drown in Ifwhere,' said the man.

159

Epilogue

*And I saw a new heaven and a new
earth: for the first heaven and
the first earth were passed away.*

——————— REVELATION 21:1 ———————

Durham, Monday 4 February 2048

8 a.m. Up in the medieval apartments of the Castle, with their view north across the roofs of Durham and on to the moors beyond, Alec's two eldest sons were having one of their usual quarrels.

'Why can't *I* be the toastmaster?' said 10-year-old Neil. 'I know how to do it just as well as Alasdair.' He said this quietly and without shouting, though it was for the fifteenth time, because, as the eldest, he had learned that reason and persistence pay – or at least an appearance of reason.

'But Mummy said *I* could be toastmaster,' cried Alasdair in anguish. No doubt he was unaware, at 9, that in another three days he would have totally lost interest in having any such function, and would not even be bothered to wonder why he had ever wanted it. But his brother's obstinacy was wearing him down, and tears were close.

'Neil,' said Jenny, also for the fifteenth time. 'I've told you again and again – don't you listen? – that's Alasdair's job at breakfast. It's his *job* and we've given it to *him* and that's an end of it. Will you please *shut up*?' Her patience too was wearing thin.

Neil, however, considered he had a right, as eldest, to all positions of responsibility, no matter how trivial. First born, first served. *Jus primi geniti.* Besides, he had a character like that of a bulldog with a slipper. Once let him get his teeth into anything and he never let go. '*Why* can't I be toastmaster? I'm older than Alasdair and I can do it better.'

160

'No, you can't, Mummy says I make very *good* toast.'

'Why do you *want* to be toastmaster, Alasdair?' said Neil, using a mode of attack that was only marginally more subtle.

'Why do *you*? You won't let me do *anything*!' Alasdair was yelling at the top of his voice, but his perception was correct.

Well indeed, why should anyone want to be 'toastmaster'? Alasdair, one year younger than Neil, tended to feel overpowered by his older, more pushful brother. He needed to be found things to do which would make him feel capable. It was an uphill task, for he usually lost interest in them anyway after forty-eight hours flat.

'You two make me tired,' said Isla, 7, loudly and distinctly. 'Why do boys argue all the time? Who'd have *brothers*?' she added witheringly, as if the term were the blackest of all possible insults.

Alec entered the kitchen, zipping up his radsuit, his mind already on the day's meetings – the chief constable with the problem of children playing in ruinous old buildings, a delegation of parents from the farming settlements around the city, and – most importantly of all, a discussion with Andy Clelland, the community's leader and inspirer, over the coming visit of the Inspectors from Edinburgh. For Alec was now headmaster of the Durham school.

'Alec,' said Jenny, 'can *you* sort out this argument? Neil *will* insist on taking over Alasdair's job.'

There followed five minutes of reasoned discussion verging on acrimony. Neil, defeated only with the utmost difficulty, tried his final throw:

'If Alasdair falls ill, can I be toastmaster?'

Well, Alasdair had won this time, but would probably have lost interest in his 'important post' by tomorrow. The dishes were dumped in the kitchen sink, and the family departed in its various directions, Alec and the three eldest children to the school, Duncan to his nursery, the baby to the creche with Jenny, who then followed the others to the main school building where she, like her husband, was a teacher. All this took only a few minutes, for the school was in one of the buildings in the Cathedral Close where, even now, most of the inhabitants of the new Durham had their flats. Only gradually were they spreading out across the

161

River Wear beyond the protection of the peninsula on which medieval bishops, the Princes Palatine of Durham, had built their great defensive walls.

'And why was that, miss? Why did we all settle on the Castle rock when we came to Durham?'

It was Jenny's morning class of 10-year-olds, whose project this term was the history of their own community – Durham reborn, one of the first steps in the resettlement of England.

'Just think about it, Mary. What have your parents told you about how things were before the settlement in the Close? Was there anyone living in the City?'

'I dinnae ken, miss.'

'Well, there wasn't, because when Mr Clelland and Mr Jamieson and I came with the first hundred settlers, the City was falling about our ears. Aye, I mean literally tumbling down.'

It had been an uncanny business, she remembered. You would get up in the morning and look out across the houses of the City, most of them roofless, rising jaggedly above the dawn mist, and suddenly one of these shadowy silhouettes would disappear, like a ghost dispelled by an enchanter. The distant rumble of subsiding masonry came to the ear, and you shivered at the eerieness of it all. It inspired a sort of fear, as if the place you were trying to revive were crumbling around you as you worked. Or you would wake up in the middle of the night with a jolt, and realise it was the sound of a collapsing building, somewhere in the deserted city below the castle mound.

'You see, Durham wasn't flattened by a bomb. They fell on Newcastle, ten miles up the road. In Durham it was the fall-out that killed everyone. So the houses were still standing, even if most of them had their roofs off. But of course there was no one living here any more. There was nothing to live on.'

And no one to do the living, save a handful of survivors scraping a subsistence from the countryside.

'But why here, miss? Why in the Cathedral Close?'

'Well, John . . .' This would have to be slow and tactful. Mary and John were two of a family of twenty, by five different mothers. A curiosity of this region of England was that since the Holocaust they produced very few male children. She supposed it was the

162

logic of natural law that had set them all living like Mormons or Muslims.

'We had to have a community, John, a place of safety where we could set up a school and an administrative centre ...'

That was not the whole of it. As the bombs had swept away power stations, factories, clothiers, chemists, schools, churches, hospitals, police and administration, so they had swept away the law. Nothing was left but scattered farms whose way of life was penurious and brutal, and whose social system was a mixture of brigandage and vendetta. The Briggses and the Washingtons, the Aycliffes and the Shadwells, for instance, had a history of feuding going all the way back to the evil days of '98. The new arrivals from Scotland, afraid they might be set upon at night and their throats cut, had settled on Cathedral Mound and fortified it for prudent reasons of self-defence.

But that was in the past. Ten years of settlement had gone by since then. Now the children from all the outlying farms were bussed in every day to their school in the Cathedral Close and bussed out every night. The River Wear had slowly taken on a different air, looking less like a moat and more like a commercial waterway with every passing summer. Civilisation had returned, with its teachers, its doctors and its judges. And what could hold more promise for the future than the confidence of little Duncan, home at half past five that afternoon from a classmate's birthday party, stumping in on his stocky 4-year-old legs.

'Did you have a nice party?'

'Yes,' replied Duncan, his eyes shining, 'and a *balloon* too.'

Alec was frowning in a preoccupied fashion when he returned to the flat that evening. 'It won't be just the Inspectors,' he explained. 'Duguid's coming too.'

'The Federal Prime Minister?' Jenny was awed, but also astonished, for the Holy Federal Assembly had never shown any interest in these English colonies, and had left it to a few private enthusiasts to settle them, run and provision them. Perhaps the government were at last, on this the tenth anniversary of their founding, having a change of heart.

'Aye, an intimidating man, so I'm told. The Holy Protestant Father. It'll be like a royal progression, he'll be touring all the new communities to find how we're making out. Morpeth, Bishop Auckland, Richmond, Ripon, Beverley, York. There's even a promise of government help — at last!'

'We'll all have to turn to and make sure to impress him, then. Well, at least he hasn't got horns!'

'Oh yes he has — so folk say!' said Alec, smiling.

'Like Moses? Goodness, it can't be true! And he didn't lead his people into the wilderness, that was *you*, love.'

'That was Andy,' said Alec, 'and without a superstition either old or new to prompt him.'

He walked over to the south-facing window and stood there, looking pensively out at the silhouette of the Cathedral, massive against the dark night sky.

'Do you remember arriving — that first day?'

'Aye, as we travelled south, nothing but mist and mist again. Then — suddenly — the Cathedral rising from the haar.'

'Like the breaking of a wizard's spell.'

'Like coming upon a lost kingdom — a forgotten city in the fog.'

Jenny joined him at the window, and they both stood gazing out into the clear darkness of the night where, high above the Cathedral's Norman towers, there floated a shifting dust of stars. From the magnetograph behind them, turned down low, came the strains of Mozart's final symphony — the Jupiter. The sky seemed almost alive and in restless movement, as its myriad pinpoints flickered upon the nebulous darkness that had brought them millions of years ago to birth. Beneath them loomed the Cathedral, empty tonight, not a glimmer showing from its windows, merely a silhouette thrown upon the phosphorescent shivering of the heavens, as if the God who dwelt there lay concealed in the most absolute darkness. A shadow hidden in a shadow.

'The dance of the atoms. I sometimes wonder — that night in Heriot Row, when Gilchrist was killed by Rimmon's carriage . . . What would have happened, if . . .'